"You want me as much as I want you,"

Gary said once they were alone in the elevator.

"I don't want any of this." Sophie sounded exasperated and more than a bit panicked.

"But you can't help yourself," he guessed.

She closed her eyes. "I can't think when you look at me like that. And I have to be able to think, Gary. I want to get through this jury duty without going crazy."

If he didn't kiss her, *he'd* go crazy. He reached out and ran his index finger along one shiny tress of her hair. The curl spiraled around his finger and he suppressed a groan. Her hair was soft and silky and incredibly sexy. "We're more flammable than any match, and you know it."

"I'd rather not know it," she confessed, once again startling him with her candor.

"Sophie," he murmured, reaching out to her again. This kiss was hot-blooded, full-throttled, the kind of kiss a man gave a woman when nothing was stopping him. Suddenly the elevator lurched to a halt and went pitch-black....

"There's a lot of me in *Courting Trouble*," says **Judith Arnold.** "I got the idea while on jury duty, sitting in the jury pool room and doing what writers do—playing 'what if?' What if I were single, and the most gorgeous guy came into the room? What if we were assigned to the same jury? I'm not single—in fact, I'm the mother of two Little League baseball stars, so all the baseball stuff Gary goes through with his son is also lifted from real life. The wedding chapel I described really exists. Novelists are always advised to 'write what you know.' Well, I certainly did that with this book!"

Don't miss Judith's exciting trilogy in Superromance—The Daddy School— beginning November 1997.

Books by Judith Arnold

HARLEQUIN TEMPTATION
561—THE LADY IN THE MIRROR
565—TIMELESS LOVE

HARLEQUIN SUPERROMANCE
611—ALESSANDRA AND THE ARCHANGEL
634—CRY UNCLE
684—MARRIED TO THE MAN
715—BAREFOOT IN THE GRASS

COURTING TROUBLE
Judith Arnold

Harlequin Books

TORONTO • NEW YORK • LONDON
AMSTERDAM • PARIS • SYDNEY • HAMBURG
STOCKHOLM • ATHENS • TOKYO • MILAN
MADRID • WARSAW • BUDAPEST • AUCKLAND

For Carolyn

ISBN 0-373-25751-1

COURTING TROUBLE

Copyright © 1997 by Barbara Keiler.

This edition published by arrangement with Harlequin Books S.A.

Printed in U.S.A.

1

GARY WASN'T SURE whether he was actually hearing footsteps or just imagining them.

It was barely past 6:00 a.m. and still dark outside. The shower he'd taken hadn't done much to invigorate him. Dressing in something more formal than his usual work clothes had been arduous; viewing himself in the mirror above the bureau had been depressing. He'd made it down the stairs without breaking his neck, not an insignificant feat since his eyes had yet to come into complete focus.

Still groggy, he was having more difficulty than usual arranging the filter in the coffee machine's basket. Hard to believe a crimped circle of paper could be giving him so much trouble. He was exhausted, he was irritable, and in the not-too-distant future he was going to have to knot the tie that dangled loosely around his collar. Neckties were his nemesis.

This was not his idea of a great day.

He heard the footsteps again—a whispery, rustly sound on the stairs. One of the dogs, probably.

He tossed some ground coffee into the basket, lost track of how many scoops he'd put in, dumped the coffee back into the can and started all over again, counting out loud. At five scoops he stopped. There were only three people living in the house, and the last time he'd asked Tim if he wanted a cup of coffee, Tim had made a face and said he considered coffee wicked gross, or something like that. Gary no longer paid close attention to his son's slang. By the time he figured out what a word meant, it usually meant something else.

The footsteps had reached the bottom of the stairs. He hoped it was Plato or Socrates. He really wasn't in the mood to be sociable with a human being.

He added water to the coffee machine and turned it on, welcoming its familiar gurgling sound. Then he opened the refrigerator. The interior bulb was too bright; it seared his drowsy eyes. Muttering a curse, he pulled an orange from the produce drawer and swung the door shut. He wasn't hungry, but if he didn't eat something, the coffee would burn a hole in his stomach.

More footsteps, approaching. It wasn't one of the dogs; their claws always made a clicking noise on the hardwood floor.

"Hey, Dad?" Tim whispered. "You awake?"

Gary turned to see his son in the doorway. He seemed to have grown another inch overnight. The kid was definitely getting too big too fast. Fourteen, and he already stood five foot nine—and if he took after Gary, he'd keep shooting skyward until he was twenty.

"Actually, no, I'm not awake," Gary answered. "Do you want some of this coffee?"

"Yeah, sure." Tim stalked into the kitchen. A year ago he'd decided he was too old for pajamas, and he looked curiously dissipated with only his underwear on beneath his floppy bathrobe. His brown hair was disheveled, but his hazel eyes were as bright as the sun at noon.

"You're drinking coffee now?" This news flash roused Gary.

"I've been drinking coffee for a long time." To Tim, a long time was anything more than fifteen minutes. "You really gonna wear that tie?"

"I really am." Gary grimaced, then shrugged. He applied a paring knife to the orange, determined to get the peel off in one spiraling strip. If he could accomplish that, he might just survive the day after all.

Tim pulled a jumbo box of cornflakes from a cabinet and filled a bowl with a mountainous portion. "You've really gotta do this, huh?"

"I've really gotta."

"Can't you just tell them you can't do it? I mean, like, things might fall apart or something while you're gone."

"First of all—" Gary smiled triumphantly as the single long curl of orange peel dropped from his knife into the sink "—things aren't going to fall apart. Your grandfather is here to keep an eye on things. And there's nothing much that needs doing at this time of year, anyway. Second of all—" he discarded the coffee grounds in the trash and poured two mugs full of coffee "—I've used up all my postponements."

"Yeah, but we're playing Acton at four o'clock today."

"I'll be there," Gary promised. He took a seat across from Tim at the old oak table, sectioned his orange and popped a wedge into his mouth. "You know what's going to happen? I'll drive into Cambridge, sit in a room all morning, get dismissed and drive home in time for lunch."

"How do you know you won't get picked?"

Gary thought about the unbroken orange peel lying in the sink. "I'm feeling lucky," he said, then consumed another wedge of orange and decided he was feeling not just lucky but downright civic. "I'm not saying I don't think your baseball game is important, Tim. But when you live in a democracy, you have certain responsibilities."

"Oh, no! Not that speech again!" Tim held his fingers crossed in front of his face, as if to ward off a vampire.

Gary grinned. "It's a good speech."

"It was good the first hundred times you said it."

"Well, today I'm doing my duty as an American—"

Tim began to hum the national anthem. Gary wadded up a napkin and fired it at him. Tim ducked, nearly tumbling out of his chair. He took a moment studying Gary's legs under the table before straightening up in his chair again. "You're wearing dungarees."

"My best jeans," Gary corrected him.

"You're wearing a necktie and jeans?"

"Do you have a problem with that?"

"Hey, not me," Tim insisted. "But I'm thinking, maybe your country might have a problem with it. I mean, this great democracy you're doing your duty to—"

"—doesn't care if I wear jeans, as long as they're clean."

"Don't you want to make a good impression?"

"If I make too good an impression," Gary explained, "I might get stuck on a jury and miss your game."

"Yeah, well, maybe we oughta grunge up your pants, then. You could go take a hike through the compost pile—"

"You," Gary scolded, "are a wise guy."

"Wisdom is as wisdom does," Tim said.

Tim's adage made no sense. Of course, at this godforsaken hour, nothing made sense to Gary. He knew farm people were supposed to be used to rising with the sun, greeting the day before the day had even begun. But despite the fact that Gary had grown up on the farm and returned to run it by the time he was twenty-seven, despite the fact that he'd managed to turn it into a profitable enterprise, he still couldn't adjust to all the trappings of farm life. No overalls in his closet. No roosters to crow him awake. No pleading for subsidies from Washington, or wearing duck-billed caps that said Cat above the visor.

"Listen, pal, there's nothing I'd rather do than sit here and watch you swallow that entire bowl of cereal in one gulp. But I've got to be in Cambridge by eight o'clock, and there's bound to be rush-hour traffic." He swallowed the last of his orange, then drained his mug and stood.

"What happens if you're late?"

"They ground me for a month. Just like what happens to you."

"Get real, Dad."

"That's as real as I get this early in the morning." He rinsed out his mug, then turned in time to see Plato and Socrates amble into the kitchen. Labrador retrievers, they were both big and brainless, but so good-natured, Gary was willing to forgive a lot.

"I've got to go," he said, scratching Plato's scruff as he passed him. "Feed the beasts, wake your grandfather if he sleeps through his alarm clock and don't miss the bus."

"Yeah."

"And fill their water dishes. Grampa always forgets."

"He doesn't forget. He just hates the dogs. He wants them to die of thirst. He says it's a slow, torturous death."

Gary laughed, and Tim joined him. He had Gary's coloring—the mahogany brown hair, the gray-green eyes, the golden skin. But every now and then—like right now, in the early-morning twilight seeping through the window above the sink—Gary glimpsed Meg in his son. Something about the curve of Tim's mouth, the pixie roundness of his cheeks...something. It was uncanny.

And Gary was obviously still half-asleep, if he was seeing Meg in his son, who everyone swore looked exactly like Gary.

He dried his hands on a dish towel. "I guess I'd better take off."

"Have fun."

"I'll see you at the game."

"You hope."

Gary slapped Tim's shoulder on his way past the table. That was all the physical affection he was allowed to show his son nowadays.

In the front hall, he picked up his keys from the mail table, used the mirror above it to fix his tie and swallowed several times to make sure the knot wasn't pressing on his windpipe. He'd hate to die of strangulation over this jury business. If only the instruction book from the court hadn't emphasized the importance of wearing clothes that "reflected the seriousness of the occasion."

So it was a serious occasion. So Gary was a good citizen. He was still enough of a rebel to wear jeans.

With a parting scowl at his reflection, he turned and headed out into the cool spring morning, as ready to do his civic duty as he'd ever be.

SOPHIE EXAMINED HERSELF in the mirror on the back of her closet door. The suit she had on was powder blue, but its severe lines, the boxy shoulders of the jacket and the below-the-knee length of the skirt, made her feel like a prison warden. Maybe a warden dressed up for Easter.

She'd bought the outfit to wear the day Mitchell had brought her home to meet his parents. It was that kind of suit.

Perfect for jury duty, she thought, spinning away from the mirror and gazing in dismay at the three dresses she'd tried on and tossed onto her bed, the panty hose she'd snagged and managed to get half in, half out of the garbage pail when she'd hurled them across the room, the four different pairs of shoes, the contents of her brown purse dumped onto her dresser and the bottle of nail polish, still open from her attempt to repair the torn stockings. It filled the room with the biting scent of acetone.

"I don't want to do this," Sophie said aloud.

She didn't want to clean up the mess. She didn't want to be wearing her grim powder blue suit. She didn't want to kill a morning in the jury room at the courthouse.

"Just go and get it over with," Lynn had urged her. "I got called last year. You sit around doing nothing till noon and then they send you home, and you're off the computer list for the next three years. Bring a book with you and pretend you're at the beach."

Sophie glanced at the stack of paperbacks on her night table. She'd stopped at a bookstore on her way home from the shop yesterday evening, figuring she would reward herself for serving jury duty by purchasing a few bestsellers to get her through the ordeal. That morning she'd sorted through them and decided none were suitable. The crime novel would make people think she was interested in the workings of the law, and then she'd surely get picked for a jury. The science-fiction book might mark her as a weirdo. The romance novel would have racy passages in it, and she couldn't imagine reading a love scene in a room packed with prospective jurors. Everyone would see her blush—something she did far too easily.

Twenty dollars' worth of paperbacks, and she had nothing to read.

"I really don't want to do this," she grumbled, shoving her feet into her navy pumps and climbing on a chair to reach the matching purse on the shelf at the top of her closet. Good Lord, she hadn't spent this much effort getting ready for her first job interview, or the grand opening of her shop, or her parents' silver anniversary party. In fact, the only time she could remember being keyed up like this was when she'd been preparing to meet Mitchell's parents.

And look at how that had worked out.

"I *really* don't want to do this," she muttered, raking the wild ash blond mop of curls out of her face and taming the more unruly strands with a couple of strategically placed barrettes. "I really, really don't want to." She reached for her telephone, punched Lynn's number and growled, "I'm going."

"Good girl. Don't worry about a thing. I'll open Simply Divine on time."

"I should be there by one o'clock. I'll want to stop off at home and change into something comfortable first. You did say they'll dismiss me at noon, right?"

"Unless you get picked for a jury."

"There are ways to avoid that, aren't there? I'll tell them the business will collapse without me—"

"It won't," Lynn said.

"And my employees will find themselves out of work—"

"All two of us."

"Maybe I can act like a dumb blonde."

"You'll have the attorneys slobbering all over you. Don't risk it."

Sophie sighed. "You're right. Guess I'll just have to get through this thing."

"Grin and bear it, Sophie."

"I'll bear it," Sophie conceded. "But no way am I going to grin."

GAZING ABOUT HER, she decided she definitely wasn't going to grin. Incredible to think that for the privilege of entering this room, where she didn't even want to be, she'd had to wait on not one, not two, but *three* lines—first, at the courthouse's main entrance, to pass through a metal detector and have her purse searched for weapons; second, at the elevator bank, where only one of the six elevators seemed to be working; and finally, at the entry to the jury room, where she was presented with an index card informing her she was Juror One, Panel Five.

The ceiling fluorescent lights blazed. The linoleum floor bore the scuff marks of the countless jurors who'd come before. The walls were covered in two-tone industrial paint, the windows overlooked one of Cambridge's less picturesque neighborhoods and the tables and chairs had probably been donated by some public high school when it refurbished its cafeteria. Sophie was all in favor of being a good citizen, but she hadn't expected to have to do it in such a dreary place.

She was lucky to have gotten a chair. The room was

packed; apparently Middlesex County was planning to start a dozen trials today. She amended that thought when she recalled that several jurors were usually dismissed for each one impaneled.

Please, God, she prayed silently, *let me be one of the jurors who get dismissed.*

Doing her best to tune out the incessant din of voices and the stale aroma of coffee combined with the equally stale aroma of a few unpleasant representatives of the great unwashed, she opened the book she'd chosen, a popular novel about a group of bitter divorcées, and buried her nose in it. It was only 8:10. In less than four hours, if luck was with her, she'd be out of here.

All around her people were drifting about. Some stood, some sat, some vanished into the hallway for a cigarette or a trip to the rest room. The court officer who'd signed her in addressed the throng through a microphone. "Welcome to the Middlesex Superior Courthouse. At eight-thirty we're going to show you a video about how the jury system works in the Commonwealth of Massachusetts. After that you'll be free to go downstairs to buy a cup of coffee. Starting at about nine o'clock or so, we'll be calling panels, so don't lose your card. Thank you for your patience."

Sophie wasn't feeling patient. She glared over her shoulder at the uniformed man, who seemed far too cheerful for her taste, and then turned back to the table and her book. And froze at the sight of the man lowering himself into the chair across from her.

Thick, collar-long brown hair framed a face of angles and shadows, dazzling hazel eyes, a prominent nose, a strong jaw and a mouth that slid easily into an ironic smile, complete with a lopsided dimple. One word lodged itself in her brain: *gorgeous.*

Aware that she was gaping, she lowered her eyes. He had on a plain gray blazer, a pale blue shirt and a horrific tie featuring a ghastly brown background dotted with what appeared to be gray kidney beans. A darting glance under the table told her he was wearing blue jeans and extremely broken-in brown loafers.

"Do you come here often?" he asked.

His voice was soft, husky, underlined with humor. It was as gorgeous as the rest of him.

Well, not the *entire* rest of him. The face was magnificent. The physique, as far as she could tell, was tall and lean and sinewy. The wardrobe, however, needed some work.

"I come here as rarely as possible," she replied, returning his smile.

He tossed a folded newspaper onto the table in front of him. It wasn't one of the two Boston dailies she was used to seeing.

"What's that?" she asked.

"A newspaper," he said, as if she were a nitwit.

To her dismay, a flush heated her cheeks. "I know it's a newspaper," she said quickly. "I was just wondering which one."

"The *Middlesex News.*"

"I never heard of it."

"We're in Middlesex County."

"I know that," she said, feeling progressively more embarrassed. "I've never heard of that newspaper, though."

"See what you learn when you get suckered into jury duty?"

She took a deep breath. There she was, seated across a table from the best-looking man in the room if not all of Middlesex County, and she was making a total ass of herself.

Another deep breath, and she regained her smile. "Suckered? Do you feel suckered?"

He shrugged. "I can think of things I'd rather be doing right now."

Sophie nodded. "I'm self-employed, and I thought that was a legitimate excuse to get out of jury duty. But they wouldn't let me off the hook. They told me I had to come."

"When your number is up, it's up." He shrugged again. Beneath his blazer his shoulders appeared broad and powerful. "I would have loved getting out of this, but they've already given me two postponements."

"Two? I thought you were allowed only one."

"The first time, they wanted me in late September. Right in the middle of the harvest. Worst time of the year for me. I asked for a postponement, and they gave me a date the first week in January. The day before I was supposed to come in, my son fell off a sled and broke his arm. I had to submit a note from my son's doctor to get out of jury duty that time. I suspect if I didn't come today they would have sent the federal marshals after me."

Sophie struggled to assimilate the influx of information. The most important fact surged to the fore: he had a son. He was a family man. She commanded herself to stop thinking about how beguiling his hazel eyes were.

"You're a farmer?" she asked, not yet ready to hear him tell her he was married.

"I've got an apple orchard. We cultivate about thirty acres of corn, too, and some other crops."

She glanced discreetly at his left hand. No wedding band. He'd said *we*, though. There must be a wife in the picture. "And you have a son?"

"Currently with all his limbs intact."

She knew she ought to ask about his wife, but she delayed the inevitable. Getting through the morning might be a bit easier if she could distract herself with a little harmless flirting. "I didn't know there were any farms in Middlesex County," she said.

"Farms, newspapers—there's a whole wide world out there," he joked. His eyes sparkled and that solitary dimple lodged firmly in his left cheek. Sophie envied his wife for being able to view his dimple on a daily basis.

The uniformed guard requested that everyone move into the next room to watch the video. The farmer stood, but instead of joining the people funneling through the doorway into the adjacent room, he waited courteously for Sophie to rise, then gestured toward the door and strolled over with her.

He has a son, she reminded herself. *He's only being polite.*

They entered a room that reminded Sophie of a church. Long, narrow rows of pews were lined up on both sides of a central aisle, with an altar of sorts—or maybe it was a judge's bench—at the front. The uniformed guard stood in front of the judge's bench, flanked by two television monitors. "Please, folks, sit as close together as you can. We've got quite a crowd this morning."

The prospective jurors slid along the pews. Sophie took a seat and her companion sat next to her. More shifting and sliding along the pew brought him dangerously close to her, his thigh less than an inch from hers, his shoulder gently brushing hers. She caught a whiff of his clean, male fragrance.

His hands were clean, too. She would have expected a farmer to have dirt under his nails—didn't they spend lots of time weeding their fields and stuff like that?—but his were spotless. On his left wrist he wore a plain watch on a leather band. Once again she noted the lack of a wedding ring.

She wished he wasn't sitting so close. She wished she wasn't so overwhelmingly conscious of him. When a straggler squeezed onto the pew, the farmer pressed even closer to Sophie, his hip nudging hers, the warmth of his body permeating her. She was grateful when the guard turned off the lights; she didn't want the farmer to see her blushing.

The videotape began. A judge and two attorneys on the tape casually chatted about the difference between civil and criminal trials, and about procedures, evidence, judges' instructions and the invaluable service the potential jurors were providing.

Sophie took it all in on one level. On another level she took in only the farmer beside her, the length of his legs, the length of his hair, the ridge of his knuckles as he rested his hands on his knees and the ridge of his jaw in profile. Along the side of her body she felt a continuing warmth, a melting heat. The man seemed to radiate waves of sensuality.

He was a farmer, for crying out loud, and Sophie was a city girl. Furthermore, he was a *father*. Just because he wasn't wearing a wedding band didn't mean he wasn't married. Who knew? Maybe he'd removed his ring when he was scrubbing his fingernails that morning, and it was right now sitting on the shelf above the sink. His wife was gazing at it and shaking her head at his forgetfulness.

Then why had he asked Sophie if she came here often? Why had he gazed at her with such blatant interest?

Maybe his leaving the wedding band by the sink at home *hadn't* been an accident. Maybe he was a sleazeball, using his morning of jury duty as an opportunity to prowl.

The possibility made her inch away from him. She bumped her neighbor on the other side, a heavyset woman who gave her a sharp scowl. Sophie smiled apologetically and inched back toward the farmer. Her shoulder collided with his, and he lifted his arm around her and rested it on the back of the pew so she would have a little more room.

It would be so natural to lean back, to cushion her head against the firm muscle of his upper arm. Sophie hunched forward.

The video ended and the guard turned on the lights. People immediately began unfolding themselves from the crowded pews, giving each other breathing room. Sophie knew she ought to put some space between her and the farmer, too. The married, philandering farmer.

But she waited until everyone else had slid out of the pew before easing away from him. It didn't seem to matter that he was a married, philandering farmer—because even if he were the most eligible of bachelors, nothing was ever going to develop from this chance encounter in a jury room.

Perhaps that was why he'd approached her. He knew as well as she did that after this morning their paths would never again cross. So what was the harm in a little playful banter?

They filed back into the other room. Fortunately, no one had claimed their chairs. "I would kill for a cup of coffee," he remarked as they headed for their table.

"If you're going to kill, this is the place to do it. There are police officers all over the building."

"Yeah. Lots of lawyers hanging around downstairs, too."

"How could you tell they were lawyers?"

The farmer smiled. "Their briefcases. Their expensive clothes. Their shifty eyes."

She grinned and shook her head. "You have to be open-minded if you're going to make a good juror."

"I'm not going to make a good juror. I'm not going to make any juror at all. I'm going to get myself disqualified as soon as possible. Listen, there's a coffee shop downstairs. If you save my seat for me, I'll buy you a cup."

She smiled. Even if he was a lecher, he was a generous one. "Thanks. I'd love some."

He dropped his newspaper onto his chair to mark it as taken. "How do you like it?"

"Cream, no sugar."

"I'll be right back."

She twisted in her seat and watched him forge a path through the crowd. She liked the way his jeans hugged his hips, and wished he'd remove his jacket so she could see more of him. She wasn't in the habit of ogling strange men, but he definitely merited ogling. In fact, she noticed at least two other women observing his passage through the room to the door and out.

Forget it, she wanted to tell them. *He's married.*

Actually, it was herself she had to remind of his status as a family man. He was strictly off-limits.

And besides...a farmer? Here in the urban sprawl of eastern Massachusetts?

True, the only traveling she'd done outside the greater

Boston area had been by airplane, so if there did happen to be major agricultural activity in the region she wouldn't know about it. As it was, she could have happily lived the rest of her life in Cambridge without ever knowing she shared the county with the best-looking farmer in the world.

Now that she knew he was in her county, his absence from the jury room left her feeling oddly bereft. She flipped through the novel she'd brought, decided she didn't want to read about embittered divorcées after all and thumbed through his newspaper. It contained little in the way of farm news. The pages were filled mostly with suburban stories— school budget woes, lawn care problems, teenage vandalism. Stories that would have made the front page of the Boston newspapers—about the mayor, or mass transit, art and commerce, everything that made cities such exciting places to live—had been buried in the back pages.

"May I have your attention, please?" the guard addressed them, his voice amplified through the microphone. "Would everyone from Panels Five and Eight please step to the front of the room?"

Sophie double-checked her index card: Panel Five.

She should have been worried about being called for a jury. She should have been panic-stricken at the possibility that she was going to get stuck sitting through a boring, protracted trial. She should have been planning her tactics to make sure one of the attorneys would reject her.

But all she could think of was that if she left the room right now she would never see the farmer again.

Which was as it should be, she told herself. Yet she hesitated, hovering near the table, gazing anxiously toward the door.

"Panels Five and Eight," the guard repeated. "Please step to the front of the room."

Around her, people rose and moved toward the counter near the door. She stood, still searching the crowds, glancing at the door, wishing she could at least say goodbye to him. It was stupid, really. He was a complete stranger. There was no need for a passionate farewell.

Except that he was buying her a cup of coffee, and she owed him a simple goodbye, at the very least.

Sighing, she walked reluctantly to the counter. "We're going to a courtroom on the seventh floor," the officer was explaining to the amassed jurors. "This is for a civil trial, and I believe they'll be requiring only six jurors and an alternate. If you don't get selected for the jury, I know it's heartbreaking, but try not to be disappointed."

This won the officer a round of derisive laughter.

Sophie forced a smile, but her gaze darted toward the door again.

"So, if you'll try to stick together—"

Please come back— she pleaded silently.

"That way no one will get lost."

—so I can thank you for the coffee....

"If you'll all just follow me—"

The farmer swept into the room, carrying two lidded paper cups of coffee. His eyes met hers, and her heart vaulted into her throat.

Before he could get close enough to pass her one of the cups, the officer stopped him. "Are you in Panel Five or Eight?"

"I'm in Eight," the farmer answered.

"Well, find a place in line. We're about to go form a jury."

The farmer rolled his eyes, then turned back to Sophie. His frown dissolved into a warm smile and he found a place in line.

Right next to her.

2

HER HAIR WAS PHENOMENAL.

It fell well past her shoulders, a glorious mass of twining, twisting silver-and-gold curls. She'd pinned it back with a few clips, exposing her delicate face and slender neck, but the hair... He wanted to touch it, to plunge his fingers deep into the coils of it, to feel its silky texture.

They were seated in a small courtroom, in individual chairs that deprived him of an excuse to nestle against her. Not that he'd had much of an excuse during the video they'd had to watch. Even though the benches had been crowded, he could have spared her a little more room.

But a man had to do something to make a tedious morning of jury duty pass pleasantly, didn't he?

That was all it was, of course—a way to pass the time. She was lovely to look at and fun to talk to, and if he could just figure out a way to guarantee that he wouldn't get stuck on the jury for this trial, he'd be happy.

A judge, two attorneys and several other people milled about at the front of the courtroom, doing their best to look important. Gary and the woman sipped their coffee in silence. An atmosphere of solemnity settled over them. He couldn't bring himself to tease her about her urban provinciality—or to say anything to her at all. No doubt she was as concerned as he about whether they'd get tied up with a trial.

She managed to cross her legs in the narrow space between her seat and the one in front of her. She had long, slim legs, and while the skirt of her suit ended below her knees, limiting his view, what he saw was terrific.

He was just fantasizing, of course. He hadn't journeyed all the way to Cambridge to pick up a lady. This particular lady would be all wrong for him, anyway. Hell, she didn't even know that Middlesex County extended beyond the city of Cambridge, an overcrowded, overbuilt, overdressed haven for upwardly mobile professionals.

All right, maybe she wasn't overdressed. Her outfit certainly "reflected the seriousness of the occasion" better than his did. The suit she wore was chic, almost too stylish for his taste, but he liked the way its color matched her pale blue eyes, and the way the shawl collar of her white blouse displayed her graceful throat.

The judge, a slate-haired woman in a black robe, gazed sternly at the twenty-four potential jurors assembled before her. "We are about to begin voir dire," she said in a gravelly voice. "That is the process by which the attorneys select jurors. Six of you will be chosen to sit on this jury, plus one alternate. We anticipate the trial to last a maximum of three days. The attorneys in this case, Mr. Harrison and Mr. Laudrey, will be interviewing you to determine who among you will sit on the jury. They are allowed unlimited challenges for cause, as well as three peremptory challenges. You must answer their questions honestly. If you lie during this process, you may be charged with perjury. Does anyone have any questions before we begin?"

Yeah, Gary thought. *How do I get myself disqualified?*

The judge turned to a man in a severe gray suit. Gary pegged him as one of the attorneys because he had set an impressive leather briefcase and a stack of legal pads down on one of the oak-veneer tables at the front of the room. He shot his cuffs, straightened his spine and gave the jurors a suspiciously charming smile. "Let me tell you a little about this trial. It's a civil proceeding involving a breach of contract between a man and a woman. More specifically, the man backed out of a marriage, and the woman is suing him for actual losses and mental anguish. A monetary award may be involved. First let me ask, is there anyone in this room who believes, for any reason, that he or she cannot be objective about this trial?"

Gary scrambled to think of a reason. Next to him the woman traced the edge of her cup with a polished pink fingernail. Her eyes were downcast, her face a picture of concentration.

If she wasn't going to disqualify herself, neither was he.

Several people did stand. An officer led them to the front of the room, where they conferred quietly with the judge and the attorneys. One by one, they were let out of the courtroom.

"I wonder what the magic word is?" Gary whispered.

The woman grinned at him. "Your Honor, I did time for murdering a judge," she whispered back.

Gary nodded. "That would probably do it."

The attorney in the gray suit turned back to those jurors who remained. "We're going to question you individually now. I'd like to begin with the first juror from Panel Five. Would that juror please step forward?"

The woman cringed. "That's me," she groaned, then handed Gary her cup and edged past him to the aisle. As she wiggled around his knees he inhaled the scent of her perfume. It smelled like the wildflowers that had taken over the fallow acres east of his house. Indian paintbrush, goldenrod, clover and Queen Anne's lace. They filled the field with a kaleidoscope of color. Yet all he could think of was blue—the woman's blue suit and her blue, blue eyes.

She crossed to the witness stand, sat and slid her tongue anxiously over her lips. Like the rest of her, her mouth was pretty, the lower lip slightly fuller than the upper. Her nose reminded Gary of Tim's nose when he'd been a baby—a rounded nub without much of a bridge. On her it looked adorable.

"What is your name?" the lawyer asked.

"Sophie Wallace," she said.

Sophie Wallace. Gary hadn't expected her to have such a name—although he hadn't really given much thought to it. Why *shouldn't* she be Sophie Wallace?

"And where do you live, Ms. Wallace?"

"In Cambridge."

"How old are you?"

"Thirty."

"You seem a little nervous, Ms. Wallace. There's nothing to be nervous about."

"I'm not nervous. It's just—I don't know, strange, being put on the spot like this." Her eyes flashed. Gary might have been mistaken, but he had the clear impression she was seeking him out in the crowd.

He smiled at her. She flickered a smile back at him.

"Do you have a job, Ms. Wallace?"

"I own a boutique called Simply Divine. We sell crafts, handmade articles of clothing, high-quality one-of-a-kind merchandise."

"Are you married, Ms. Wallace?"

"No," she said. Gary's smile widened. He shouldn't care about her marital status, but the fact that she was single permitted him to indulge his imagination—about her lips, for instance, and her pink tongue, and her legs, and her hair...

"Have you ever been jilted?" the lawyer asked.

She looked affronted. "I beg your pardon?"

"Have you ever had your heart broken by a man?"

"That's a very personal question!" She turned to the judge, apparently looking for assistance.

"I'm afraid it's relevant to the trial, Ms. Wallace," the judge informed her. "All the jurors will be asked similar questions."

Sophie Wallace sank in her seat and mulled over her answer. Once again her gaze settled on Gary. He shrugged sympathetically, although he was far more interested in her answer than he had any right to be.

"Well," she finally said, a feisty glimmer lighting her eyes, "I'm sure it must seem hard to believe, but yes, there have been a few men who actually failed to swoon at my feet."

Several of the jurors chuckled. The lawyer frowned. "Ms. Wallace, this is a serious litigation."

"And that was a serious answer. Do you honestly think a single woman in America can reach the age of thirty without getting shafted by a guy at least once? Nuns, maybe, but not the rest of us."

"Ms. Wallace—"

"I mean, let's face it, we're talking about American men.

How many normal, red-blooded American men put women's feelings ahead of their own? Why do you think women are stronger than men? We've got to be if we're going to survive the treatment we get from all the jerks out there who pass themselves off as men."

Two women among the jurors began to applaud. The judge banged her gavel. "Ms. Wallace, please. No speechifying."

"Well, Your Honor—*you* know what I mean, don't you?"

The judge wrestled with a smile and lost. She looked away for a minute, and when she turned back her expression was once again austere. "Mr. Harrison, have you any other questions for this juror?"

He regarded Sophie warily. She stared back. He sighed. "We'll accept for now."

The judge looked to the other lawyer, whose attire was every bit as expensive looking as Mr. Harrison's. He was grinning. "No objection."

"Very well," the judge said to Sophie. "You may be seated."

Sophie smiled, obviously relieved, and climbed down from the witness stand. A court officer intercepted her on her way back to the empty chair next to Gary. Taking her arm, he steered her toward the jury box.

She froze. "Wait a minute! Does this mean I'm on the jury?"

"Yes, Ms. Wallace," the judge informed her. "Please take a seat."

"But—but—what about my store?"

The judge peered down at her. "What about it?"

"If I have to sit through this trial—"

"No *if* about it, Ms. Wallace. You *do* have to sit through this trial."

"But what if my store goes out of business?"

"I highly doubt that will happen. This won't be a long trial, Ms. Wallace, and like Mr. Harrison and Mr. Laudrey, I have every confidence in your ability to serve. Please take a seat now."

Sophie let out a long breath. Her shoulders slumped. She looked as if she were considering all her options—and concluding that she didn't have any options at all. Grudgingly, she let the officer lead her to the jury box.

Gary felt for her. He, too, worried about what would happen to his business if he got stuck on a jury. Of course his father could run the farm—he'd run the farm just fine throughout Gary's youth. At this time of year the work consisted of plowing, fertilizing and irrigating, and getting the retail stand set up for the season. Gary could afford to serve on this jury if he had to.

What was he thinking? A trial would foul up his life! Not only the farm but Tim needed him. The baseball season was just beginning to rev up. How could Gary concentrate on a trial if he was missing the opening innings of his son's games?

Well, it would be only for three days. That was what the judge said. Three days.

Three days on a jury with an unmarried, thirty-year-old boutique owner named Sophie Wallace.

Not exactly the worst fate in the world, he decided, foolishly hoping the jury wouldn't fill up before they called his number.

SOPHIE WATCHED as the next few potential jurors were questioned. Two were accepted, three were challenged. For the life of her, she couldn't guess why some made the cut and some didn't. The two lawyers, Harrison and Laudrey, seemed to rely on intuition more than anything else.

A chubby woman in a bright red dress was selected. A silver-haired grandfather was rejected. A man who identified himself as a "sandhog"—a construction worker who specialized in digging underwater tunnels—was accepted. A pimple-faced fellow barely out of adolescence was excused. Juror by juror, Panel Five was winnowed down until none was left—and three jury seats remained to be filled.

She observed the farmer. He sat quietly, balancing their two cups of coffee and watching the judge, the lawyers, the jurors being questioned and those being seated. Occasionally his gaze intersected with hers, and she felt a jolt of... She wasn't sure what. Expectation? Empathy? Hope.

Please, she prayed, *if I've got to sit through this trial, let him get stuck sitting through it with me.*

She couldn't keep obsessing about him; she had too much else to worry about. Like Simply Divine, for instance. Lynn could manage the store, but she couldn't handle the appraisals of merchandise that freelance artisans brought in for sale.

And what about Sophie's blind date? She was supposed to have lunch with a friend of Lynn's boyfriend tomorrow. Not that Sophie particularly relished blind dates, but her social life had been so sluggish lately she'd let Lynn talk her into meeting the man. According to Lynn, he was a financier or banker, something to do with investments. He was witty and cute and he owned a summer house on Martha's Vineyard. Lynn had sworn Sophie would instantly fall love with him.

Well, she was on a jury. She'd have to instantly fall in love with him after this trial was over.

She sighed, wishing she could drink the coffee the farmer was holding for her. Really, that was the only reason she wanted him to get picked: so she'd have access to her coffee.

Sure, she thought wryly—and pigs flew.

The juror undergoing questioning, a dapper middle-aged man with a Haitian accent, was found acceptable by both sides and joined the growing jury. The next two jurors were both rejected, and then a prim older woman, the sort Central Casting would send to the studio for the role of a spinster librarian, was accepted. Only one seat left to fill.

"Panel Eight, Number Four," the court clerk intoned.

The farmer stood, still balancing the two cups. He gazed around, apparently looking for a place to put them. No convenient surface offered itself, so he carried the two cups to the witness stand at the front of the room, set them carefully on the polished wood molding that bordered the chair and took a seat.

Mr. Harrison glanced at the coffee and sniffed in disapproval, then studied the farmer intently. Sophie studied him, too. She wanted him to wind up on the jury. She wanted it so much, she was shocked by the intensity of it.

"What is your name, sir?"

"Gary Brett," he said in that husky, unbearably sexy voice of his.

"How old are you, Mr. Brett?"

"Thirty-seven."

"And what is your occupation?"

"Farming."

Harrison's eyebrows twitched and his nostrils narrowed. Evidently he didn't think much of farmers. "Are you married, Mr. Brett?"

"No."

Sophie hadn't realized she was holding her breath. Now she let it out slowly, carefully, so no one would notice how curious she'd been about his answer. He wasn't married. He wasn't a cad who'd left his wedding band on the edge of the sink in the hope of picking up a woman in the jury room.

"Have you ever been in a bad relationship?"

Unlike Sophie, Gary Brett didn't seem the least bit rattled by the question. Perhaps that was because he'd been expecting it; all the other jurors had been grilled on their romantic history.

He leaned back in the polished oak chair and regarded the lawyer with a smile. "Sure," he drawled.

"Were you devastated by it?"

His smile widened. He looked absurdly confident, as if impervious to devastation of any kind. "Sure."

"Can you imagine a circumstance in which you would jilt a woman?"

"I suppose I could."

"No further questions," Harrison said. "No challenge."

Maybe the lawyer had no further questions. But Sophie was overflowing with them. Why could he imagine a circumstance in which he would jilt a woman? What sort of circumstance? Why had he answered so nonchalantly? Had he, in fact, jilted women? Had his wife left him or had he left his wife? Did he have custody of his son, or had the boy merely been visiting him last January when he'd hurt himself sledding?

None of your business, she chided herself.

The other lawyer, Laudrey, took over the questioning. "A farmer, Mr. Brett," he said, smiling unctuously. "What an interesting career."

"Someone's got to do it."

"What do you grow?"

"Fruit, corn, vegetables and some annuals and perennials."

"It must be hard work."

"At least as hard as lawyering," Gary remarked dryly.

Laudrey had the good sense to smile. "Have you ever been the one to end a relationship with a woman?"

Gary gave the question thought. "I don't think these things are ever one-sided. One person may make the move to end it, but it's usually because you've got a mismatch, or you don't see things the same way. If you're asking whether I was ever the one to make the move, yes. I was."

"Was the woman hurt?"

"We were both hurt."

It dawned on Sophie that Gary Brett wasn't trying terribly hard to get out of serving on the jury. His answers were too fair, too reasonable. If she'd been asked questions like his, she could have easily come up with outrageous answers and gotten herself rejected. Either he actually wanted to be picked for the jury, or else he was too decent to maneuver his way out of it.

"Mr. Brett, what do you think is the man's responsibility in a relationship?"

Gary stared the lawyer straight in the eye. "Honesty."

"Anything else?"

"Sure, lots else. But honesty is the main thing. Everything else springs from that."

Sophie sighed. Gorgeous, honest and unmarried. The man was too good to be true.

He had lousy taste in clothes, she reminded herself. And he had a son. And he was a farmer, living so far from Cambridge he read a newspaper she'd never even heard of. He wasn't perfect. Far from it.

And this was a jury, for crying out loud. Just because they'd exchanged a few friendly words, and he'd bought her a cup of coffee, and he had bedroom eyes and a physique to die for, and when he'd sat beside her during the video she'd felt as if her very soul had melted into a puddle of yearning...

He was nothing to her. Really.

"No objections," said Laudrey.

Gary Brett stood, shook down the legs of his jeans and lifted the two cups of coffee. An enigmatic smile crossed his lips as he stepped down from the witness chair and turned toward the jury box. His gaze sought hers, caught it and held for a fraction of an instant—just long enough for Sophie to acknowledge him with a smile of her own.

He followed the clerk to a seat in the jury box. He would have had to lean across several people to hand Sophie her coffee, and she was glad he didn't bother. It was probably cold by now. And if her hand accidentally brushed against his, she knew she would embarrass herself by blushing the color of a fire engine.

The judge dismissed the remaining few jurors, thanking them and explaining that an officer would escort them back to the waiting room. Once they were gone, the judge turned to the seven selected jurors. "Only six of you will actually decide this case," she told them. "One of you will be an alternate, in case a juror is unable to fulfill his or her obligations due to illness or some other emergency. All seven of you will hear this trial with the assumption that you will decide it. Not until you enter into deliberations will you know who the alternate is."

Sophie listened closely to the judge's words. Yet one tiny part of her mind was tuned to a different channel. That one small brain fragment couldn't care less that the judge was a no-nonsense woman with fierce eyes, and that the two lawyers in their conservative suits and glossy tasseled loafers made her think of Tweedledum and Tweedledee, and that this trial was going to revolve around broken promises and broken hearts.

One stubborn sliver of consciousness clung tenaciously to a single thought: for the next three days she was going to be with Gary Brett.

HE COULD TELL HIMSELF a million times he'd done nothing deliberate to get himself chosen for the jury. But the moment the second lawyer, Laudrey, accepted Gary, he'd felt a sense of triumph all out of proportion to what had occurred.

What had occurred, he pointedly reminded himself, was precisely what he had hoped wouldn't occur when he'd left the house at sunrise that morning.

Once the jury selection was completed, the seven jurors were sworn in. "You may talk among yourselves when you're not in the courtroom," the judge instructed them. "But you may not discuss anything that might bear even tangentially on the trial. You may not talk about any of the evidence presented or voice your thoughts and opinions until the deliberation stage. Before the trial begins, you will be expected to select a foreman from your ranks. Any questions?"

Someone asked whether they would be allowed to take notes during the trial. After the judge answered their questions, they were allowed a few minutes to make telephone calls to tell anyone who needed to know that they weren't going to be home by midday.

When it was his turn to use the phone, Gary called his father and promised to do his best to catch at least the last few innings of Tim's game. "You'll be there, won't you?" he asked.

"You bet I will. At least *some* of us have our priorities straight."

"Pop, it's not like I won the lottery here. I didn't ask for this." He didn't mention the momentary exhilaration he'd experienced at the prospect of spending a couple of days in the company of Sophie Wallace.

"Did you tell the judge you've got a son who plays on his school's junior varsity team?" his father asked.

"If I had a son who was still in diapers I'd have trouble getting excused. A fourteen-year-old son sure as hell won't do the trick."

"How about if he gets in trouble at school?"

Gary cursed under his breath. "What happened?"

"Nothing. I'm saying just suppose."

"Do me a favor, Pop—don't give him any ideas. I'll be home later. Cheer him on for me at the game, okay?"

"I'll do that."

"And feed the dogs, would you?"

"Maybe."

"Pop!"

"I said maybe. What have those mutts ever done for me?"

"Pop—"

"Go sit on your jury. I'll break the news to Tim when he gets home from school."

Two jurors were still waiting their turn to use the phone when Gary was done. He headed down the hall to the courtroom, discreetly loosening the knot of his tie so he wouldn't choke. Adjacent to the courtroom was the jury room, a drab, windowless conference room consumed by a Formica-topped table, a dozen chairs, a coffeemaker, a blackboard and little else. Entering, he found a few jurors gathered around the coffee machine. Sophie wasn't among them.

He couldn't let on that he took a special interest in her. Shaping an impassive smile, he moseyed over to the machine to get a cup of coffee.

The sandhog glommed on to him. "Jack Reilly," he introduced himself.

Gary shook his hand. "Gary Brett."

"Farming," Jack said, his dark eyes narrowing on Gary. "I never met a real farmer before."

"I never met a real sandhog before. I'm not even sure what a sandhog is."

"Tunnel digger. I'm working on the Central Artery project. This trial couldn'ta come at a better time. The work's a bitch, but they gotta pay me my union wage as long as I'm sitting on a jury. How about you?"

"I won't starve."

"Your farm gonna shrivel up and die while you're here?"

"No. Apple trees have a way of growing even if no one is hovering over them."

"Hi." He heard her voice behind him, light and crystalline, and felt another unjustifiable surge of pleasure. Turning, he found himself gazing into her eyes, as light and crystalline as her voice.

"Hello, Sophie." He liked the way her name felt on his tongue.

"And you're Gary."

"I'm Gary." Damn. Her eyes were too blue, unbelievably blue. The suit enhanced their color, reflected it, turned it deep and soft and true. True blue.

And he was transforming into a sentimental drip, which was definitely not like him. "This is Jack Reilly," he said, drawing the man beside him into the conversation. "He's a sandhog."

"So I heard."

An officer stood in the doorway. "Folks, you'll have to choose a foreman now. The trial will be starting in a few minutes."

Jurors guzzled their coffee and discarded the waxed-paper cups in a metal trash can near the blackboard. Then they gathered around the table and studied each other.

Never one for false humility, Gary spoke up. "If no one else wants the job, I—"

"I want it," Sophie said.

He frowned at her. Even though she was wearing high heels, he had a few inches on her, and he angled his gaze downward, hoping to cow her.

It didn't work. "Who says we can't have a forewoman?" she posed. "I'll do it."

"I just think..." *I just think I prefer to be in charge of every situation,* he said silently. It happened to be true, but as a campaign speech it wouldn't win him much support. "I think I've got the negotiating skills necessary to be a foreman."

Sophie returned his stare unflinchingly. Despite her magnificent hair, her willowy build, her long, golden lashes and her lush, feminine mouth, she was tough. He sensed her obstinacy in her posture, the thrust of her chin, the flint in her gaze. "I've got plenty of skills, too," she said, more to him than to anyone else in the room.

"Yes, but I'm..."

"Bigger than me," she conceded, then turned to the other jurors with a broad smile. "I own and manage a successful store. I—"

"And I own and manage a successful orchard."

"You work with weeds. I work with people."

"We all heard your speech about men during voir dire, Sophie. Frankly, I'm surprised you were even allowed to sit on this jury after sounding off like that. You're not exactly objective."

"I'm as objective as anyone else in this room," she argued. "We've all had our hearts broken at least once. That's why we were picked. We've all been either the jilter or the jiltee. Some of us have probably been both." She sent Gary a ferocious scowl.

"I shall be the forewoman," the spinster-librarian announced with such resounding finality, no one dared to contradict her. Gary suspected that if anyone did, she'd spank them with a ruler. "My name is Miss Prinz. Not *Ms.*, but *Miss.*" She turned to the officer at the door. "We're ready."

He opened the door connecting the jury room to the courtroom. Head held high and shoulders squared, Miss Prinz led the jury around the table toward the door, reminding Gary of a mother goose leading a gaggle of obedient goslings.

Two goslings weren't quite so obedient. He and Sophie hung back, watching the other four jurors trail Miss Prinz through the door.

He glared at Sophie. She glared back. "I hope you're happy," he muttered, motioning toward their strict, prissy leader.

"It's your fault," Sophie retorted. "You should have let me be the forewoman."

"Well, you know how it is. We normal, red-blooded American men fail to swoon at your feet."

"Yes," she said, a twinkle of humor lurking in her eyes. "Sometimes you fail to swoon, so I have to resort to tripping you." With a saucy grin, she turned from him and strode to the door.

Gary watched her departure with a mixture of amusement and dismay. He noticed the twitch of her hips, the flex of her calf muscles, the bounce of her long, thick hair. He smelled her wildflower fragrance and heard her lilting voice echoing in his head.

And he wondered whether she'd tripped him without his even realizing it.

3

"IN THIS TRIAL," Laudrey was saying, "certain issues are uncontested. A verbal contract was agreed to by my client, Jocelyn Kramer, and the defendant in this suit, Ronald McGuire. Mr. McGuire breached this contract. No one disputes this.

"What is in dispute is whether Mr. McGuire should be required to compensate Ms. Kramer for her losses, which—as you will see during the course of this trial—were catastrophic. She abandoned her home and her career when she moved to New England to be with the man who had promised her his hand in marriage. She expended a considerable amount of time and money in the intricate planning of their wedding day. She gave and gave, she sacrificed and sacrificed, and on a whim, Mr. McGuire decided to break the contract.

"There is no question he was within his rights in breaking that contract. Contracts are broken all the time. The only question before you, ladies and gentlemen, is whether Mr. McGuire owes my client something for the pain and suffering he has caused her."

As Sophie listened to the lawyer's opening statement, she felt long-dormant emotions quiver to life inside her. She'd thought this was just a legal proceeding, not something so personal, something that cut so close to the bone. Good God, Mr. Laudrey could have been talking about her!

Was she blushing? And if she was, could Gary Brett see it? And if he did, could he guess why?

He was seated beside her, for no other reason than that they'd been the last two jurors to enter the courtroom. The jury sat in two rows, four in front and three—the sandhog, Gary and Sophie—in back. They'd been supplied with pencils and pads, and as Laudrey described his client's plight, Sophie's fingers fisted so tightly around her pencil, she nearly snapped it in two.

She had thought the only problem her jury duty would pose was that she'd have to be away from her store for a few days. It turned out the real problem was that she'd have to relive the most stressful, painful period of her life—because, just like Jocelyn Kramer, Sophie had once been on the wrong end of a broken contract.

Ancient history, she told herself, hoping her face didn't give her away. After all, she'd recovered. It was just a bad memory, fading like an antique photograph so that, three years later, the color was all but gone, the outlines barely visible.

She loosened her death grip on the pencil and scrutinized the judge, who sat regally in her elevated seat, gazing down at the court. Sophie wondered how one went about signaling a judge and requesting removal from the jury after the trial had begun. She had to disqualify herself. She couldn't possibly hear this case fairly. She wasn't trying to weasel her way out of jury duty, but she simply couldn't listen to a suit about a woman who'd been jilted when she herself had endured a similar humiliation.

On the other hand, the lawyers had asked her about past heartbreak during the voir dire, and she'd answered honestly. She hadn't gone into detail, but they hadn't asked her to. If either of them hadn't cared for her answers, they could have challenged her.

They'd asked everyone else on the jury about past heartbreak, too, she recalled. Each of the jurors seemed to have a sad story to tell. The plump woman in the red dress, the sandhog, the aggressively Miss-not-Ms. Prinz...and Gary Brett. Even Gary Brett had had his share of bruising run-ins with the opposite sex.

Seated beside her, leaning back in his chair and stretching his legs as far as he could in front of him, he looked far too strong and confident to have ever had his heart stomped on. Surely he must have done the stomping.

She would have to remember that when her daydreams started running away with her. Instead of marveling at his hypnotic hazel eyes, the thick, tawny hair that swept over his collar, his rugged profile and his lean, lithe build, she ought to keep reminding herself that, even though he'd claimed he'd been devastated by a bad relationship, he'd said it with a smile. He'd also said he could imagine a circumstance in which he would jilt a woman.

Sure. He could probably imagine lots of circumstances. He'd probably jilted dozens of women in his day. Probably his wife had walked out on him because he'd broken her heart—and maybe others', even while he was married. He was probably a creep, a thousand times more selfish and insensitive than Mitchell.

She shot a quick glance his way. Dear God, he was too handsome to be a creep.

All the more reason to assume he *was* a creep. The better looking they were, the more they got away with.

She forgot about getting herself removed from the jury. So what if she couldn't be perfectly objective about a case like Jocelyn Kramer's? There was no such thing as perfect objectivity. And if Sophie convinced the jury to strike a blow for wounded women everywhere by voting a huge award for the plaintiff, she would consider having served at this trial one of the highlights of her life.

"HELL HATH NO FURY like a woman scorned," said Harrison. "You've heard what Mr. Laudrey has to say. My client, Ronald McGuire, informed Ms. Kramer shortly before they were scheduled to be married that the marriage would be a mistake. Of course it hurt her. Of course it was awkward. Mr. McGuire could have spared her the momentary sting of rejection on that day—and instead married her and subjected her to the far greater agony of a divorce. He could have spared her a fleeting embarrassment, and embarrassed her twice as much by divorcing her within days or weeks of their marriage.

"Instead, he chose the honest, honorable course. He called off the wedding before it took place.

"Yes, Ms. Kramer was scorned. Yes, she is furious. But does this personal drama belong in a courtroom? When all is said and done, ladies and gentlemen of the jury, we hope you will find in favor of a man who did the honest, honorable thing and spared both Ms. Kramer and himself the ignominy of a failed marriage."

Gary adjusted his lanky legs more comfortably in the tight space between his seat and the row in front of him. He knew he was supposed to be hanging on every word the lawyers said. But by the end of the two opening statements, he had a pretty clear idea that this trial wasn't going to wade into any life-and-death issues. No one had been defrauded out of millions of dollars; no one was going to spend the rest of his life in a wheelchair. No one had been fired, assaulted or vandalized.

All that had happened was a wedding got canceled. Hurt feelings shouldn't be dealt with in court. When you got ditched, your best recourse was to go home and lick your wounds for a while, or go to the local watering hole and drink heavily until a friend drove you home because you were in no condition to drive yourself, and the next morning you were supposed to wake up with a whopping headache and say, "She wasn't worth it."

Or, in light of the particulars of this suit, "*He* wasn't worth it."

Gary was a veteran of a few nasty breakups. He was also a veteran of what, all in all, had been a damned good relationship. He and Meg had had their spats, their sulks, their full-blast rip-roaring altercations. But they'd also had their love, and love—not a wedding, not a heap of sacrifices and compromises, not pride or any of the rest of it—was what had kept them together. And if she'd had worn her seat belt that night eight years ago, love would probably still be keeping them together through the rip-roarers and the brooding silences.

But Meg had always been a stubborn fool about certain things. Like seat belts.

There were plenty of ways to lose one's lover. Compared

to the way Gary had lost Meg, a flame-out with one's intended just hours before the wedding seemed trivial.

Harrison rambled on for a while, in the manner of a professional who was used to being paid by the hour. When at last he had finished his opening statement, the court was recessed for lunch. The judge instructed the jurors to be back in one hour.

Jack Reilly, the sandhog, turned to Gary and whispered, "Do we have to pay for our own lunches?"

"I guess so," Gary whispered back, then turned and filed out of the jury box behind Sophie. He wondered what she was planning to do about lunch. Would she be interested in eating with him? Were two jurors permitted to eat together without the rest of the jury chaperoning them? What was the etiquette in this sort of situation? What was the legality of it?

In the jury room, a court officer advised them, for the sake of convenience, to make use of the cafeteria downstairs. "Let me remind you that you are not to discuss anything about this trial until you enter deliberations. And no, the court isn't required to reimburse you for your food expenses unless the trial lasts more than three days," he told Jack Reilly, who seemed miffed.

"There's no such thing as a free lunch," Gary quipped, his gaze trailing Sophie as she moved toward the door. She hadn't given him a look since they'd left the courtroom. He didn't know whether that was because she was concentrating on the opening statements or because she blamed him for her failure to become the jury forewoman.

He noticed that Miss Prinz had left the room with Sophie. If he didn't make a move soon, Sophie would wind up having lunch with prissy Prinz and he'd wind up eating with

Jack, who didn't seem like such a bad guy, although he was liable to spend the entire hour complaining about having to pay for his meal.

Fortunately, whatever elevator problems had existed that morning hadn't been fixed, and Gary easily caught up with Sophie and Miss Prinz at the elevator bank. He sidled up to Sophie. "Any chance you're free for lunch?" he murmured, hoping Miss Prinz wouldn't hear. She seemed like the sort who would tattle on them to the judge.

Sophie turned. Her eyes were gentle, her smile hesitant. "I still owe you for that cup of coffee."

"Believe me, I'm keeping track of every penny. After today, I start charging interest."

"Gary, I—"

An elevator arrived, already crammed with passengers. Gary took Sophie's arm, nudged her in, wedged himself in beside her and sent an apologetic smile to Miss Prinz and the other waiting jurors as the door creaked shut.

He expected Sophie to berate him for his pushiness—or else to thank him for having maneuvered her into the first elevator to come along. She said nothing, though. Her eyes straight ahead and her hands clutching her purse, she stood rigidly, her elbows pressed to her sides, and nibbled her lower lip.

It occurred to Gary that he'd like to nibble her lower lip, too.

She remained silent throughout the ride downstairs and the stroll down the hall to the cafeteria. The line at the cafeteria counter was short, although by the time the other jurors made it downstairs it was sure to extend out the door. Gary congratulated himself silently for having gotten Sophie and himself into the overcrowded elevator.

He handed her a tray and gestured for her to step ahead of him. She studied the array of foods that lined the counter, then selected a cup of yogurt and a bottle of juice.

"Is that all you're going to eat?"

"I'm not that hungry," she said.

"I was willing to spend as much as three dollars on you," he told her as he lifted a ham sandwich onto his tray. "I'll forgive the interest, too."

"Big spender," she joked, though her laughter sounded forced.

Something was bothering her. He wondered whether that something was him.

They found a place to sit at the far end of the room, near a window overlooking the traffic on Thorndike Street. The table was small, adequate for two people but no more. He saw three other jurors join the line near the door and hoped they wouldn't drag chairs over and join him and Sophie, at least not until he found out what was bugging her.

She spent a long time spreading a paper napkin across her lap, opening the container of yogurt and stirring the fruit up from the bottom, transforming the creamy white fluid to pink. Gary waited her out. If she was really upset about his having challenged her for the position of foreman, she was free to leave him and join the other jurors, who were gathering at a larger table in the center of the cafeteria.

She didn't leave him, though. She simply stirred her yogurt with the kind of single-minded intensity Gary generally associated with sports, and maybe prayer.

"Your store will survive."

She flinched and glanced up. He hadn't realized how wide-set her eyes were. They seemed even wider now, round with surprise. "What?"

"Your store. I'm sure it will be fine."

"Oh. I'm sure it will, too." She gave him another tentative smile.

Evidently that wasn't what was troubling her. Still, he was glad to have gotten a conversation started, and he wasn't going to abandon the subject now. "Remind me what the store's called and what you sell there."

"Simply Divine. Stuff." She laughed faintly. "Handcrafted items. Pottery, jewelry, wall hangings, clothing…"

"Stuff" was right. Gary couldn't imagine shopping at Simply Divine. It didn't sound like a place where one would find lumber, wheelbarrows, bushel baskets—the sort of items that topped his shopping list.

"I'm sure it'll be fine," she said again. "My friend Lynn is also the store's manager. She'll keep things running smoothly until I get back."

"Then why are you a nervous wreck?"

"I'm not a nervous wreck!"

She'd just spent the past five minutes stirring her yogurt, and her face was as pink as her food. She could protest all she wanted, but Gary knew a nervous wreck when he saw one.

Maybe he should try to console her. "There's really nothing to worry about. The trial's going to take only a couple of days. Though for the life of me, I can't imagine how they're going to stretch it out past today. I mean—"

"We're not supposed to discuss it," she cautioned him. Her cheeks grew rosier and her eyes rounder.

"Something's bothering you about it, though."

"It's a sad situation, that's all. I feel sorry for both parties. But really, Gary, I don't think we should talk about it. Tell me about your son instead."

She dug into her yogurt, and he relented, partly because her appetite seemed to be returning and partly because she was right about their not talking about the trial. "His name is Tim," he told her. "He's fourteen."

"Does he live with you?"

"Yes."

She slid another spoonful into her mouth. Gary watched the way her lips pursed around the spoon, the way her pointy little chin moved, and her throat. She was only eating, but the motions of her lips were so unintentionally arousing he found himself dreaming of smearing yogurt across his chest and having her lick it off. And across his belly, and his legs, and his—

"Fourteen must be a difficult age," she said.

"Difficult is one way of putting it," he muttered, having more than a bit of difficulty locating his voice. He bit into his sandwich and banished all thoughts of yogurt and anatomy from his mind.

"Are you worried about his being home alone while you're here?"

"He'll be in school till three o'clock. And he isn't exactly alone when he's home. My father lives with us, as well as a couple of dogs."

"Do you have livestock?"

"It's not a ranch. It's an orchard."

"Yes, but even so... I thought you might have chickens or something."

"Chickens are nasty animals. I'd never raise them. Cows are kind of cute, but pricey. If you're going with a dairy, you've got to own a big enough herd to justify all the equipment. And to raise cattle, you need grazing land. It's just not practical in these parts, unless you're going for some sort of boutique meat or something."

"Boutique meat?"

"Organic, or high-protein feed or something. Meat you can charge a fortune for. It just isn't a practical crop in Massachusetts."

"Orchards are practical?"

"They're a ton of work, but we've got the right climate for them here. Corn does well, potatoes, squash, tobacco—"

"Tobacco?" This time when her eyes grew round, it was with fascination.

Gary chuckled at her reaction. His father used to grow tobacco, but the demand for the crop had diminished over the years, and by the time he was in high school, Gary had been urging his father to discontinue it. He wanted his father to grow healthy crops. He'd been quite the self-righteous prig in those days.

"Cigar tobacco," he informed Sophie. "Wrapping tobacco—broad-leaf. Way back when, it was a big crop in Massachusetts." He swallowed another bite of his sandwich. "You aren't from around here, are you?"

She shook her head. "I grew up south of San Francisco, in Carmel. I don't know if you've ever heard of it—"

"Of course I've heard of it."

"I guess it got pretty famous when Clint Eastwood was elected mayor."

"I knew about Carmel long before Clint Eastwood took office." Gary shook his head and laughed. "You think I'm a hick, don't you?"

"Well..." She did him the kindness of looking sheepish. "You *are* a farmer, and you were reading that weird newspaper."

"The *Middlesex News* isn't a weird newspaper. It's a fine newspaper. And as for being a farmer, I know this will come as a shock to you, Sophie, but we've got electricity, indoor plumbing, cable TV—you name it. There are farms in California, too. Agriculture is one of your state's biggest industries."

"I know." She sighed, then mirrored his smile. "I've just always lived in cities."

"Carmel isn't a city."

"It's a town."

"I live in a town, too. It's called Stow, and it's got a shopping center and a post office and the whole shebang. It's even got some things that Cambridge doesn't have. Like peace, and open roads, and rolling hills. Trees. Silence."

"I'd go crazy in a place like that," she confessed. "I love the city, all the jazz, all the noise. All the people—I just love it. My folks live in Austin now, and even that's a little too quiet for me."

"Austin, Texas? Too quiet?"

"Some of us are city mice and some are country mice," she explained, polishing off her yogurt and washing it down with a sip of juice.

As troubled as she'd been when they'd boarded the elevator, she seemed to have recovered fully. Her eyes danced; her hair glinted in the overhead light. She looked relaxed and amused and breathtakingly pretty.

And she was a city mouse, and he was a country mouse. He'd prefer to think of himself as a fox, or maybe a stallion—although setting a proper example for Tim didn't allow for much in the way of stallion behavior. But the bottom line was, he was country and she was city, and in two more days they'd both go back where they belonged and never see each other again. He'd return to his peace and silence, and she'd return to her noise and jazz.

Two days. Maybe less. So what if her nervousness had made him want to gather her in a hug and whisper that everything was going to be all right? So what if sitting beside her in the jury box made him want to loop an arm around her, to lift her hair away from her face and press his mouth to the pale, soft skin behind her ear? So what if, despite the cafeteria's bright lighting and chattering patrons, Gary discovered that gazing across the table at Sophie Wallace made his heart beat a little faster and his jeans feel a little tighter?

Two days of pointless temptation. If he were really a mouse, he'd keep his distance.

But he was a fox, a stallion. A man. He reached out and brushed his fingers lightly across the back of her hand. "I think our time is up," he said.

She started slightly at his touch, her eyes flashing, her tongue darting out to moisten her lips. But she didn't pull her hand away. "Is it?" she asked, sounding oddly breathless.

"By the time we get an elevator, it'll be almost an hour since the judge recessed us."

"Then we'd better go."

He skimmed his fingers across her hand again, and then he withdrew. He was playing with fire—and getting himself absurdly overheated, considering that all he'd done was give her a friendly little pat. He and Sophie were jurors. He couldn't let himself feel anything when it came to her.

She lowered her gaze uncertainly, studying her hand as if she thought he might have left a mark on it. Then she lifted her eyes to his again, and he saw emotion in them: panic, excitement, regret. Yearning.

Whatever he was feeling, she was feeling it, too.

By FOUR-THIRTY, when the judge recessed the trial for the day, Sophie was exhausted. They'd listened to Jocelyn's mother testify about the elaborate wedding she and her daughter had planned. Although Jocelyn lived in Lexington and Ronald McGuire in Boston, the ceremony was to have taken place in a small town west of Boston, in an historic chapel built by Henry Ford. After the ceremony, Jocelyn and her new husband were supposed to have traveled in a horse-drawn surrey down the road to an even more historic inn to celebrate their marriage with a sit-down dinner for two hundred people. According to Mrs. Kramer, Jocelyn and her bridesmaids had spent a total of more than six thousand dollars on their dresses. Flowers had been ordered, a photographer and musicians hired, hotel rooms reserved for the one hundred and twenty-three guests arriving from out of town, and on and on. By Mrs. Kramer's reckoning, the wedding that never was had cost Jocelyn and her parents upward of thirty thousand dollars, not including airfare.

And on the morning of the wedding, less than two hours before the ceremony was about to begin, as Jocelyn was being shoehorned into her thirty-one-hundred-dollar antique-replica wedding gown with seed pearls hand-stitched across the bodice, Ronald McGuire had suffered a sudden change of heart.

Sophie was glad her relationship with Mitchell hadn't gotten as far writing a check to a caterer or lining up a minister. Her parents could never have afforded a posh wedding on her father's salary as a professor of studio art and her mother's minuscule earnings as a quilter, but Mitchell's family would have wanted an extravaganza along the lines of what the Kramers had arranged. Still, hearing Mrs. Kramer enumerate the financial losses involved in her daughter's aborted wedding made Sophie want to shed a few tears.

Losing money was bad enough. Losing all one's dreams was far worse. If the case had gone to the jury that afternoon, Sophie would have demanded millions of dollars in reparations from that beast McGuire.

The judge admonished the jurors not to talk to anyone about the trial overnight, or even to think about it. "We'll resume at 9:00 a.m. tomorrow. I urge you all to be here promptly." With a bang of the gavel, Sophie and her fellow jurors were released for the day.

Her head ached from the afternoon's testimony, with its deluge of numbers and its undertone of grief. Her neck was stiff and her fingers were smudged with graphite from the copious notes she'd jotted onto her pad. Worst of all, her soul seemed somehow out of whack.

Partly it was the empathy she felt for the plaintiff and her mother. But mostly it had to do with Gary Brett.

She had tried to fend him off over lunch—or, more accurately, she'd tried to fend off her own attraction to him. She knew she couldn't be more than a diversion to him, a way for him to entertain himself when he wasn't in the courtroom.

But whenever she looked at him, or sensed his presence next to hers in the jury box, or heard his husky voice, she found herself caught in a whirlpool of thoughts and longings. He was tall and strong and handsome. He was single. He was raising a son and taking care of his father and growing crops, and he had dogs. It was almost hilariously wholesome.

Yet the way her body had been jolted by the light, casual stroke of his fingers against her hand hadn't been the least bit wholesome.

She was overloaded. Short-circuiting. How could she juggle a futile attraction to her fellow juror with her memories of the total hash she'd made of her life the last time she'd been involved with a man? Not that she was involved with Gary, not that she would ever want to be involved with him, but...

But why did she keep thinking of his son and his dogs and his apple trees, his open roads and rolling hills, his silence, his peace?

Silence made her edgy. Peace was boring. Dogs slobbered. Open roads led nowhere. She would be wise to remember that.

She stood in the jury room as her fellow jurors swarmed about, collecting their things and chatting. Rolling her head from side to side, she massaged the knotted muscles at the back of her neck. If she was lucky enough to catch a cab the instant she stepped outside the court building, she could go straight to the store and put in an hour before closing time. But cabs were never around when she needed them, and she would want to change her clothes and wash her face before she had to deal with her customers.

Sighing, she poked through her purse for her wallet, calculated that she had enough spare cash for a cab and snapped the purse shut. "Need a lift?" Gary asked.

She jumped. He had a way of sneaking up on her—and she had a way of overreacting to him whenever he did. "A lift?" she echoed, sounding ridiculously dazed.

"You said you lived in Cambridge. I can drop you off on my way home, if you want."

If she wanted? It was her dream come true. "Thanks, but I'll catch a cab," she said. Letting him drive her anywhere would be an invitation to disaster. She might start fantasizing about his work-roughened fingers caressing the back of her hand, and about the edge of his jaw showing a hint of whisker at the end of this long day, and about his dogs and apples and all the rest. She might start talking about the trial, which was a definite taboo.

"Really, I don't mind," he said.

The plump woman in the red dress waved to Sophie and shouted, "See you tomorrow!" She and Sophie had come upon each other in the ladies' room, and she'd told Sophie that sitting on jury duty was the most exciting thing she'd ever done.

Sophie waved back. "See you, Louise."

"I'm parked in the garage down the block," Gary said. She wondered if anyone could hear them, if she and Gary could get in trouble for fraternizing outside the courthouse, if they'd become the subject of gossip throughout the judicial system.

For God's sake, accepting a ride home from an acquaintance was hardly worth the breath it would take to gossip about. The drive would take only about ten minutes. It would give her time to slip into some comfortable slacks and flat-soled shoes before she went to the store to spell Lynn.

"Okay," she said. "Thanks."

As soon as she saw his smile, she was overcome with misgivings. This was a mistake. She was getting to like him too much. He was being too nice to her, and she was too willing to accept his benevolence.

Yet her mouth curved into a matching smile, and she fell into step beside him as they left the jury room.

They rode downstairs in another crowded elevator. Several policemen, three lawyers and two seedy young men wearing T-shirts promoting heavy-metal bands pressed together in the small car. The lawyers spewed legal jargon in low, somber voices. The heavy-metal kids smelled of stale cigarette smoke. One of them wore an earring shaped like a skull; the other had a tattoo on his arm of a rose impaled on a stiletto, with blood dripping from the petals.

Sophie gritted her teeth and tried not to lean against Gary. But when the tattooed boy jostled her, she had no choice. The wool of Gary's jacket was softer than she would have expected, and his chest was harder, taut with muscle.

His hand drifted to the small of her back in a protective gesture. He wasn't making a pass at her, any more than he'd been making a pass at her when he'd touched her hand in the cafeteria. But his palm felt seductively large and warm against the curve of her waist. Powerful. Possessive.

Don't think about it, she ordered herself. *Don't think about him. He's a man who offered you a ride. A juror. A farmer wearing a bad necktie.*

As soon as the elevator door slid open she bolted from the car. Gary easily kept up with her. He yanked the knot of his tie loose, then slid off his jacket and hooked it over his shoulder. "They'd better fix the elevators before some claustrophobic maniac freaks out," he remarked.

Perhaps that was his way of communicating that he hadn't really intended to place his hand on her back, but that he'd had no choice because she'd pressed herself against him—which he knew she hadn't intended to do, but she'd had no choice.

And perhaps she was overrationalizing everything.

Leaving the courthouse building, she felt herself unwind as the real, unprocessed outdoor atmosphere of an April early evening wrapped around her. The air was mild, carrying the familiar scents of automobiles and brick and cooking aromas wafting from a few neighborhood restaurants. Out west in farm country, where Gary lived, the air no doubt smelled like grass and bugs and mulch.

Most people would probably find those rural smells more appealing than the hot, tangy perfume of urban life. Sophie wasn't most people, though. She felt at home in the heart of downtown Cambridge, surrounded by buildings and fire hydrants, asphalt and traffic.

She and Gary strolled side by side down the block to the parking garage. Gary bypassed the elevator for the stairs and Sophie happily followed. She'd spent enough time cooped up in sluggish elevators for one day.

On the second level he held open the stairwell door for her, and she preceded him into the garage area. She spotted a middle-aged pickup truck parked at the end of one row. Gary started toward it.

It figures, she thought. Farmers would be likely to drive

trucks. She should be grateful he hadn't offered to tow her home on the back of a tractor.

To her surprise, he stopped several cars before they reached the truck, and unlocked the door of a shiny Saab hatchback. "This is your car?" she blurted out.

He grinned. "I guess it must be. My key fit in the door."

"It looks brand-new."

"Four years old. I paid Tim a fortune to wash and wax it last week." He held open the door for her.

She lowered herself onto the leather seat and tucked her legs into the space below the dashboard. In the half minute it took him to amble around the car to the driver's side, she made note of the car's immaculate interior, the maps neatly arranged in a door pocket, the rear seat uncluttered, the floor vacuumed, the gear stick adorned with a polished walnut knob.

Gary arranged himself behind the leather-wrapped wheel and smiled at her. "What?"

"What do you mean, what?"

"You look stunned."

"I was expecting something different."

His smile grew quizzical. "What were you expecting?"

"I don't know. A truck, I guess. With a load of manure in the back."

"I usually do carry manure with me wherever I go," he confirmed, tongue firmly in cheek. "But I figured with all those lawyers, the courthouse would have an ample supply of the stuff."

"You don't think much of lawyers, do you?" Sophie said as he backed out of his parking space.

Gary shrugged. "I'll grant that they serve a function. But

when all they're doing is raking in fees and wasting our time
filing suits over broken engagements—"

"Don't talk about it," she cut him off.

He pressed his lips together and nodded. "You're right."
He steered down the ramp to the exit, paid the attendant and
merged with the traffic on Spring Street. "You'll have to give
me directions."

She told him to turn right at the intersection, and he did.
"We're going to go straight about a mile and then make another right turn," she said. He nodded again.

They rode in silence, as if afraid to venture into any discussion that might bear on the trial. Gary focused on the traffic and Sophie focused on him. His eyelids were lowered
against the setting sun. His hands were relaxed on the wheel.
At a red light he unbuttoned his cuffs and rolled his sleeves
up a couple of turns. His wrists were bony, very male.

If the silence in his part of the county was peaceful, this silence wasn't. Not because of the cars around them, the pe-
destrians jaywalking and the T trains shuttling overhead, but
because of the undercurrent of awareness humming between Sophie and Gary. Without his farm to concentrate on,
or his son, or the trial the judge had ordered them not to
think about, her mind was left to ponder the man beside her,
his long legs, his mussed hair, his rumpled shirt and loosened tie, his callused fingers—fingers that had brushed
against her hand and ignited sparks of desire through her
body. She studied his mouth, quirked in an ironic smile, and
wondered what it would feel like against hers. She observed
the lean contours of his chest, the breadth of his shoulders,
his flat abdomen, and wondered whether he'd attained his

virile build through diligent exercise or simply through the daily labor of farming.

She remembered the way his hip had nudged hers on the bench that morning. The way his palm had felt against the small of her back. And his fingers, stroking her hand so casually, he couldn't have meant anything by it...and yet her body had responded and was still responding at the memory of it. She wanted to feel him caressing not just the back of her hand but the inside of her wrist, the crease of her elbow, the nape of her neck. Her cheek, her throat, her collarbone, and lower...

She shifted in the bucket seat and averted her face so he wouldn't notice her blushing. What was the matter with her? Would he have offered her a lift home if he'd known she would be casting him in her own private X-rated fantasy?

"Make a right at the next corner," she mumbled.

"Hmm?"

She turned back to him. "A right at the next corner."

He shot her a quick look. "Is something bothering you?"

Yes, something was bothering her. She was seated beside a perfect gentleman whom she had shamelessly reduced to a sex object in her mind. "Nothing," she lied. "I'm just...tired."

"You're a beautiful woman," he said.

Her face grew hot. She turned away again. "Don't say that."

"Why shouldn't I say it? It's the truth."

"Gary, we have to serve on this jury. We can't let anything get in the way of that. It's important. It's our job as citizens. And—"

"When you live in a democracy you have certain responsibilities," he completed.

"You sound like you've said that before."

"A million times or so, to my son," he admitted, grinning. "Believe me, I understand our responsibilities. All I did was comment on your appearance. The normal reaction would be to say, 'Thank you.'"

"Thank you." She sighed. "You're making me uneasy."

"No. You're making yourself uneasy. Why can't I say I find you attractive without your making a big deal out of it?"

"Because..." She sighed again. She could repeat her speech about their being good citizens, or she could remind him that she was a city mouse, or she could drum up any of a number of other reasons. But none of them seemed very valid to her at the moment. "I just can't get through jury duty if I think you're..."

"Coming on to you? I'm not," he said. "I won't. All I said was that you're beautiful."

His tone said much more. In the husky rumble of his voice, in the light burning in his eyes, he was communicating far more than a simple compliment, and she knew it.

Gazing at him, she knew he knew it, too.

"That's where I live," she whispered, gesturing toward the quaint brick-faced town house that contained her apartment.

He pulled to the curb and yanked on the parking brake. When he reached for the lever to open his door, she reflexively put out her hand to stop him. Her fingers curved around his forearm, now bare below his rolled-up sleeve. His skin was warm, dusted with a light webbing of hair.

"Don't get out," she said.

She meant to remove her hand from his. She honestly did. But all of a sudden, it seemed, he had rotated his hand and captured hers, weaving his fingers through hers and imprisoning her with his stare. "You feel it, too, don't you?"

She felt awareness vibrating between them in the close confines of the car. She felt drawn to him. She felt her rationality slip away.

"I don't think this is a good idea," she managed.

"Which idea? I've got about a thousand of them. I hadn't settled on one yet."

Slowly, so slowly she couldn't find it in her to protest, he leaned toward her, closing the distance between her seat and his, her face and his. "*That* idea," she murmured an instant before he kissed her.

Damn. Not only was Gary more handsome than any man had a right to be, not only did he have a seductive voice and an irresistible smile, but he could kiss. Superbly. Sublimely. With such understated eroticism that she had to restrain herself from squirming in her bucket seat.

And that was with his mouth closed.

She might as well have been a stick of butter in the sunlight, softening, melting, dissolving into a pool of sensation. Just the pressure of his lips against hers, gentle but persuasive, made her want to moan, made her want to climb over the gear stick and settle in his lap. She forgot to breathe; she forgot *how* to breathe. All she could think of was that she'd never been kissed like this before, by a man like Gary. It didn't matter that he was practically a stranger, that he lived a life totally alien to her, that he was wearing a repulsive tie, that they were serving together on a civil trial jury—

Yes, it *did* matter. Good Lord, it mattered! For all Sophie knew, they could get arrested for this! Surely there was a law forbidding jurors from kissing after court had been dismissed for the day! Marshals would come and clamp handcuffs on them and lead them off to jail—she to the women's penitentiary and Gary to the men's. They wouldn't be able to see each other for years, let alone finish what Gary had started with one overwhelming kiss. She would have to wear an orange canvas jumpsuit, and she'd lose Simply Divine, to say nothing of her reputation. And Mitchell's parents would grin smugly and say, "See? Didn't we say she was all wrong for our son? Cream rises, and she's fallen. And now she's rotting in jail because she consorted with a farmer."

"No," she groaned, reacting to her own bizarre nightmare.

Gary apparently assumed she was addressing him. Just as well, she thought, collapsing against the leather upholstery of her seat as he pulled back. She gulped in a shaky breath and closed her eyes, trying to will her heart to stop pounding like a pile driver.

"Sophie?" His voice was a bit ragged around the edges.

"That was *definitely* a bad idea," she said.

He laughed softly. "Maybe I should try one of the other nine hundred ninety-nine ideas I've got."

"No. You shouldn't." Opening her eyes, she groped for the door handle and gave it a yank. "Thanks for the ride," she mumbled, gathering up her purse and hurling herself out of his car before he had a chance to act on any more of his ideas.

Not until she was inside the vestibule of her building, with the outer door shut firmly behind her, did she peek through the glass to see if he was gone. His shiny midnight blue Saab remained at the curb for a few minutes, then peeled away and drove out of sight. Only then did she let out her breath.

Never in her life would she have guessed that jury duty would turn out to be such a personal trial.

tightened at the curb for a few minutes, then backed away and drove once more. Only now did she feel for real the pent-up tension. [text partially obscured]

4

"WHAT'S WRONG?" Tim asked.

Gary spun around from the sink, where he'd been rinsing out his coffee mug. Nothing was wrong, absolutely nothing. It was seven-thirty, the sun had left a glaze of pink across the dawn sky and life was full of promise. Gary had fixed a pot of coffee, let the dogs out to answer nature's call, let the dogs back in and filled their dishes with food and water. He'd donned fresh jeans, a crisp shirt and a necktie, he'd consumed two cups of coffee and a banana and he would soon be on the road, cruising to Cambridge, to the courthouse, to the jury box.

To Sophie Wallace.

The way Tim was gaping at him from the kitchen doorway put him on guard. "I give up," he said carefully. "What's wrong?"

"You were singing," Tim accused.

"Me? Singing in the morning? Not a chance."

Tim sauntered into the kitchen, using his foot to nudge Socrates out of his path. The dog didn't spare him a glance, but continued munching noisily on the kibble in his dish. "I heard you humming," Tim insisted. "It sounded like something from an Eagles CD. One of those real old songs." To Tim's way of thinking, "real old" meant anything that predated his own birth.

Maybe Gary had been humming—and if he had been, he surely wouldn't have been humming a song that became popular *after* Tim was born, because by definition any song less than fourteen years old was dreadful. He had to admit being unnerved at the thought that he could be humming so early in the morning—and without even realizing it. But he was happy. He was going to see Sophie. Why not hum?

"It's like, yesterday you thought jury duty was gross. And today—"

"I never said it was gross," Gary argued. "I said it was my duty as a citizen."

"And you missed my game. I hit two singles."

I got to first base, too, Gary thought, recalling the kiss he'd shared with Sophie before he'd dropped her off. He remembered the softness of her lips, the softness of her sighs, her soft, feminine fragrance...and his memory of all that softness made him the very opposite of soft.

He hadn't lived the life of a monk in the years since Meg died. But no woman had tempted him quite the way Sophie did, with her shiny, silky hair, her animated blue eyes and her high-voltage personality. No woman had intrigued him quite the way she did, bristling with indignation one moment and lapsing into reflection the next, erupting in musical laughter or lively chatter and then hunching over her court-provided notebook, scribbling furiously as the lawyers tested the limits of verbosity.

Maybe Gary ought to hang around with city mice more often. The women he met in Stow were solid and simple, concerned with property taxes and school board elections and the weather. He understood such women; he could relate to them. But they didn't keep him awake at night, under relentless hormonal siege.

"I'm sorry about missing your game, Tim," he said, shaking the excess water from his cup and placing it in the dish rack to dry. He disguised his grin as Tim matter-of-factly filled a clean mug with coffee for himself, as if he'd been starting his day with a cup-a-Java for years. "Your next game is Saturday, right? I'll be there."

"I probably won't hit two singles again," Tim lamented, setting down the mug and scrutinizing his father. "That tie is grotesque."

Gary peered down at the tie. It featured a bright red background across which spread a colorful print of football helmets with the professional team logos on them. "You gave me this tie for Father's Day," he reminded Tim.

"Four years ago," Tim shot back. "I was just a kid then. I had no taste."

Gary eyed the scruffy young teenager—still just a kid in his father's loving view. Tim was wearing green paisley boxer shorts, a beige pocket T-shirt and his baggy bathrobe. He was not exactly a fashion plate, himself.

But Gary didn't care whether his son approved of his apparel. He was going to see Sophie, spend the day with her, sit beside her in the jury box and maybe steal second base before the afternoon was through. Tim's insults couldn't dampen his mood.

He chucked Tim in the shoulder, swatted Socrates' tail-wagging rump on his way out of the kitchen and grabbed his keys from the mail table in the hall. He was already outside on the front porch before he realized he was humming "Life in the Fast Lane." At this godforsaken hour, he actually was singing.

And it was all Sophie's fault, he thought with a smile.

SOPHIE ARRIVED at the courthouse with only a few minutes to spare. Those few minutes were rapidly consumed by a delay at the metal detector inside the front door and then another, longer delay waiting for an elevator. Like yesterday, only one of the building's six elevators was functioning, and a familiar assortment of people—lawyers, policemen and punks with assorted jewelry piercing and tattoos adorning their bodies—stood ahead of her in line for that single working elevator. By the time she reached the jury room, the hands on her watch had moved a couple of ticks past nine o'clock.

But the trial hadn't started yet, and the room was crowded with her fellow jurors greeting each other and sipping coffee from the electric pot on the side table. As Sophie stepped across the threshold, all of her tension about running late strained out of her like water through a colander, leaving behind a different kind of tension—a warm, restless yearning that shivered deliciously inside her the instant she spotted Gary Brett.

He was leaning against the table that ran the length of the narrow room, a paper cup of coffee in his hand left and the sandhog yammering into his right ear. He appeared less than enthralled by the sandhog's monologue. The moment she entered the room, he straightened his spine and pushed himself to his feet. The corners of his mouth quirked upward, flashing that mischievous dimple of his as his eyes met hers.

Well, why shouldn't his attention be on her? Her attention

hadn't strayed far from him since he'd driven away from her town house the previous late afternoon. It was his fault that she'd suffered from insomnia all night, his fault that she'd been too edgy to eat breakfast, his fault that she'd tried on three different outfits before settling on the salmon-hued tunic and pencil-thin black skirt she had on. It wasn't the dowdiest outfit she owned—that honor belonged to the matronly blue suit she wore yesterday—but she couldn't wear her usual clothing around Gary Brett. Most of her skirts ended a couple of inches above her knees; most of her tops were scoop-necked and sassy. At least this blouse had a mandarin collar, and the skirt fell to midcalf. If only it didn't have a thigh-high slit, barely held shut by a few cloth-covered buttons that failed to hide much.

Judging by the way Gary's gaze slithered down from her hair to the lightly shaped shoulders of her tunic, to its straight hem below her hips and then to that confounded slit in her skirt, she would guess the word *dowdy* hadn't entered his mind.

If he could be so obvious about checking her out, she could check him out, too. She could amuse herself with an inspection of his hair, his seductive hazel eyes, his dangerously dimpled smile, his drab corduroy blazer, his tie—

Good God. She'd thought the tie he was wearing yesterday had been wretched. This one was worse.

Evidently farmers didn't know the first thing about neckties. She supposed she ought to be relieved that his tie featured only football helmets and not something worse, like pitchforks and silos, or piglets and slop. The football motif was hideous, though. Blindingly bright team logos screamed from an even brighter field of red: Green Bay Packers! Tampa Bay Buccaneers! New England Patriots!

It was too gaudy, too hectic...too *much*. But then, better to gawk at Gary's ghastly tie than at his hypnotically appealing face.

He set down his coffee and said something to the sandhog before starting toward Sophie. Just watching his long, confident strides carry him across the room was enough to trip alarms in her mind, and an even more alarming heat deep inside her. Last night her memory of him hadn't been an exaggeration. He really was as devilishly handsome as she'd imagined. Maybe more handsome.

Before he could reach her side, a clerk appeared at the door connecting the jury room to the court. "Do you all have your notebooks?" he asked. "Does anyone need a pencil? We're about to begin."

Miss Prinz, the jury forewoman, sidled up to Sophie, who courteously mouthed a good-morning. Miss Prinz gave her a bloodless smile and remarked, "I noticed you took prodigious notes yesterday."

If she'd noticed that, she'd probably also noticed how much Sophie had blushed during the opening statements. Perhaps she'd noticed that Gary had caressed Sophie's hand at lunch, and that she'd left the courthouse with him when the trial had been recessed for the day. *She knows*, Sophie thought guiltily. *She knows there's something going on between Gary and me.*

She ought to respond to Miss Prinz's comment, but her mind was a jumble of disjointed thoughts. Gary was lurking just out of her range of vision; she could feel his nearness, off to her left. His presence was like an electromagnet too close to a credit card, scrambling any coherent data her brain might have held.

Miss Prinz was waiting for her to say something. "I like taking notes," she managed, such a feeble remark she was afraid Miss Prinz would chastise her—or worse, rap her across the knuckles with a yardstick.

The officer rescued her from the forewoman's scowl by signaling that it was time for the jury to enter the courtroom. "Please use the same seats you sat in yesterday," he ordered them.

Sophie sighed, pleasure and dismay battling inside her. The seat she'd sat in yesterday was next to Gary.

"Good morning," he murmured, coming up behind her.

She knew, from the tingling warmth in her cheeks, that she was blushing again. As if his nearness weren't enough, hearing his voice reminded her too vividly of those minutes they'd spent enclosed in his car, when he'd told her he had a thousand ideas—and acted on one of them. She didn't need to ask what the other nine hundred ninety-nine were; the husky undertone of his voice offered a clear hint of what rating those ideas would receive from the Motion Picture Association of America.

"Good morning," she mumbled, focusing on his tie in the futile hope that his lack of sartorial flair could immunize her against him.

She filed into the second row of seats in the jury box, Gary right behind her. Taking her seat, she crossed one leg over the other, then realized her mistake: positioning her legs that way caused the slit in her skirt to gap. She hastily uncrossed her legs, pressed her knees primly together and smoothed the black fabric over them.

Jocelyn Kramer and her lawyer were seated at their table, the would-be bride looking forlorn yet determined. Sophie experienced a surge of sympathy for Jocelyn, especially after observing how cocky and smug her ex-fiancé appeared as he lounged at his table across the aisle. As if jilting a woman was an admirable thing to do, as if the woman he'd once promised to love forever was nothing more than a nuisance to him.

Before Sophie lost all her objectivity, she locked her gaze onto the judge's vacant bench. The officer who'd led the jury to their place stepped forward and announced, "All rise..." and the judge swept in, her black robe swirling grandly around her.

Once she had settled into her thronelike chair, the jury resumed their seats, as well. Folding his lanky body into the seat beside Sophie, Gary accidentally brushed her leg with his knee. At least, she assumed it was accidental. His legs were too long for the narrow space between the two rows, and he had to contort himself to fit.

He brushed her with his knee again, letting her know that the first time hadn't been an accident, after all. She turned to glare at him and lost herself in the shimmer of his eyes.

The metal detectors downstairs might be good for finding traditional weapons. But Gary Brett would never need to pack a gun. His gaze was lethal. And its firepower was augmented by that rakish dimple she was growing to hate because she adored it so much.

"This morning," the judge announced, rescuing Sophie from her overheated thoughts, "we will be taking a field trip."

Excitement rippled through the jury box. Gary stared at

the ceiling and snorted in disgust. Sophie, however, was too curious about the trip to be annoyed. A field trip might prolong the trial, but Lynn had assured her that Simply Divine was not going to go bankrupt in her absence. If a field trip was part of the trial, Sophie had no choice but to accept it. She was going to be as diligent a juror as she could be, given that she was probably undermining the nation's entire legal system by entertaining erotic fantasies about a fellow juror.

"This trip should take a total of two hours. We will travel to the site of the aborted wedding ceremony. The plaintiff believes that only by seeing the chapel and the inn where the reception was to have taken place will the jury have a full sense of the loss incurred by the plaintiff."

"Ooh, isn't this terrific?" exclaimed Louise, the juror who had claimed yesterday that sitting on a jury was one of the great thrills of her life. "I wish I'd brought my camera!"

"Yeah," Gary muttered under his breath, his tone dripping with sarcasm. "This is one of those moments I'd want to preserve for eternity."

Sophie kicked him to silence him. It wasn't a hard wallop; she wasn't trying to inflict pain. She only wanted him to behave.

Yet signaling him that way was so...intimate. And why shouldn't she give him an intimate kick? He had kissed her, after all. It had been a relatively tame kiss, at least as far as the mechanics, but it had been enough to make her want him to kiss her again...enough to make her want him to do a hell of a lot more than kiss her.

The tie, she reminded herself. *He's a hick from the sticks, with a kid and two dogs and a tie with football helmets all over it.*

None of that seemed to matter when he directed his simmering gaze her way. She would guess she looked pan-icked—she certainly *felt* panicked. But he looked as smug as Ronald McGuire, the other acknowledged heartbreaker in the courtroom. Gary smiled with self-satisfaction, as if her gentle kick implied everything she feared it did and he con-sidered those implications just peachy. Or apple-y, given the kind of farmer he was.

Gary Brett had broken hearts, she reminded herself. He was a father, so there had to be an ex-wife in the picture somewhere. He had undoubtedly broken her heart. Probably he'd broken his wife's heart just by looking at her—or, heaven forbid, by looking at another woman the way he was looking at Sophie right now.

Squaring her shoulders, she turned from him and stood. The bailiff was signaling the jurors to follow him. A field trip would be just what Sophie needed: fresh air, the clear light of day and a picturesque chapel and inn to remind her of pre-cisely what it could cost a woman to fall for the wrong man.

THE SCHOOL BUS, with Middlesex County Court painted on its sides, featured seats wide enough for two adults. It took very little maneuvering on Gary's part to wind up seated next to Sophie. She didn't object, didn't protest, didn't smile politely and inform him that she wanted to sit with Louise across the aisle. She simply shifted as far from him as her seat belt would allow, and stared out the window.

He made her anxious. So, big deal. She made him anxious, too. He just happened to be better at hiding it.

Maybe *anxious* wasn't the right word. Sitting next to her charged up his nervous system in a way that wasn't exactly unpleasant. As the bus rumbled west along Memorial Drive, the spring sunshine sifted through her hair, making it swirl with silver and gold highlights. Precious metals, he thought, although he knew that if he touched the wild tumble of curls, they wouldn't feel like metal at all. They would be soft and silky, and he would plow his fingers into the thick mass and find himself unable to resist kissing her again.

They were under scrutiny, though, not just by their fellow jurors but by the court officers positioned strategically throughout the bus to make sure none of the jurors broke the rules that had been painstakingly explained to them before they'd boarded. They were not to discuss any aspect of the trial. They were not to comment on their impressions of the chapel or the inn. Once they arrived at the site, they were prohibited from speaking at all, although they were allowed to take written notes. During the drive, they were permitted to talk among themselves, but only about matters totally unrelated to the trial.

The fierce sexual undercurrent flowing between Gary and Sophie was totally unrelated to the trial, but he doubted the court stenographer occupying the seat in front of them would agree if they talked among themselves about that particular matter. "The river looks pretty, doesn't it?" he remarked, resorting to inanities.

Sophie seemed reluctant to face him. She turned slowly in her seat, until she was facing forward, displaying her slender neck and pointy chin and little-girl nose in profile. "Yes, it does." She addressed the back of the stenographer's head.

"Have you ever been to one of the Esplanade concerts?" He gestured toward the park that extended along the opposite shore of the river, the grass still shaking off its winter slumber and the trees just beginning to bud with new leaves.

The morning air was clean enough to highlight the Hatch Memorial Shell, the park's outdoor amphitheater.

"No. I hear those concerts always draw a huge crowd. The Boston Pops concerts attract half a million people, don't they?"

Gary nodded. "On the Fourth of July, they attract something like that. Not that Tim would care one way or another about the Boston Pops. They sometimes hold free rock concerts there. Last summer he begged me to take him to some free punk-band show. But a few years ago, a riot broke out during another free rock concert. No way was I going to let him go."

"Does he live full-time with you?"

"As opposed to what? Shipping out for six months a year with the navy?"

"As opposed to..." Her cheeks darkened to the same salmon shade as her blouse. "Really, I have no right to ask."

"That's okay. Ask anyway." He was delighted that she was interested enough in him to be nosy.

"Well..." She wove her fingers together in her lap. Her hands were slender, her fingers tapered and her skin milky smooth. They were a pianist's hands, or maybe an artist's. "Even in this day and age, it's not that common for a father to get full custody of a child."

"It is if the mother is dead," he said softly.

She looked stricken, her complexion growing pale. Then she looked contrite. Then she looked guilty. He was tempted to tell her she had no need to apologize for trespassing on his past, but he liked the idea that he'd jumbled her emotions. He wasn't going to unjumble them for her.

"I'm so sorry," she said.

Most of the time, he felt uncomfortable when people treated him with overweening delicacy, regarding him as somehow noble because Meg had died. But Gary wasn't about to complain. Let Sophie give him a few nobility points for being bereaved. Let her desire to comfort him, to ease his pain. He could think of lots of delightful ways for her to accomplish that.

The truth was, she looked as if she was the one in need of consoling. She remained unnaturally pale; her eyes glistened with moisture and her hands fidgeted in her lap. If the court stenographer hadn't been sitting right in front of them, if blabbermouth Louise didn't have a nearly unobstructed view of them from across the aisle, he would have closed his hands around Sophie's and murmured that everything was going to be all right, that he would make it better for her—or let her make it better for him, if that was the way she wanted to deal with it.

Holding hands would not do. He shoved his hands into the pockets of his blazer, instead. "Don't feel bad," he said, smiling. "You couldn't have known."

"Was it—did it happen recently?"

"Eight years ago."

"How tragic for your son. To lose his mother so young...."

Enough was enough. This was definitely getting uncomfortable. Much as he wanted the many consolations Sophie could offer, he didn't want her pity. "My son is fine," he insisted. "He's a happy, normal kid, as strong as a bull when he isn't falling off sleds and breaking bones."

She peered into his eyes, as if unsure whether to believe him. Well, hell, he wanted to declare, he'd endured his sorrow and he'd gotten past it, and he was now as happy and normal as his strong-as-a-bull son. And when it came to male-female type situations, he was no longer in mourning, and hadn't been for quite some time.

He could think of no way to communicate that without sounding either unforgivably heartless or inexcusably presumptuous, or both. It wasn't as if Sophie hadn't already figured out that he had the hots for her. He'd kissed her, and he had every intention of kissing her again, once they'd escaped the prying eyes of the Middlesex County Superior Court. Being attracted to Sophie Wallace had nothing to do with Meg. He'd loved Meg, he would never forget her—but she had been dead a long time, and he was alive.

He was scrambling to think of a diplomatic way to express this when the bus swerved sharply onto the turnpike's entrance ramp, tossing Sophie against his chest. He looped an arm around her shoulders, even though her seat belt would have kept her from tumbling into his lap.

The bus took another sharp turn, and she braced herself with a hand against his knee. Her palm curved against the muscles of his thigh, and he imagined her hand on his body, his jeans miraculously disappearing so she could touch him skin to skin. Her hair dusted his chin and he caught an intoxicating whiff of her flowery cologne, and he imagined a whole lot more.

The instant the bus straightened course, she withdrew from him, flushed and flustered and adorably breathless. "That driver is a maniac," she muttered.

"No, he's not. I paid him to do that," Gary joked.

Sophie stared at him, obviously shocked. Then she mirrored his smile and relaxed. "You're a naughty man."

"I try my best." They'd apparently moved beyond the sad

stuff, and Gary relaxed, as well. "So tell me, how does a city slicker from a little town like Carmel wind up in the Hub?"

"The Hub is Boston, isn't it?" she asked. "I live in Cambridge, not Boston. I'm not exactly a city slicker, Gary. I'm just...urbane," she said, then nodded, obviously pleased to have come up with the right word.

"So how'd you get from Carmel to Cambridge?" he asked.

Her blush returned, making her look absurdly young and innocent. She glanced out the window, but there was no river to capture her attention, only the dreary asphalt and ugly buildings lining the turnpike.

With a sigh, she turned back to him. "I really can't go into it."

"I told you my life story. You have to tell me yours."

"You didn't tell me your life story," she argued quietly. "And I *can't* tell you mine."

"Why not?"

She motioned toward the stenographer, then shifted uneasily in her seat. "We'd wind up discussing the trial," she whispered.

Her life story would lead them to a discussion of the trial? Aha. That was interesting.

He tried to make the connections on his own. Carmel to Cambridge, California to Massachusetts. Marriage? A forfeit of big bucks? A frivolous lawsuit?

"Are you divorced?" he guessed.

"No. Please don't ask, Gary—"

"Got a boyfriend?"

Despite her blushing, she pursed her lips. "None of your business."

"I'd like to make it my business."

"That's the ugliest tie I ever saw," she said, abruptly changing the subject. "I thought the tie you had on yesterday was the ugliest tie I'd ever seen, but now I realize how wrong I was. This one's worse."

He peered down at his chest and laughed. It was ugly, all right—but in a robust sort of way. "It was a Father's Day gift from Tim."

"Oh...I'm sorry," she said, immediately retreating.

The magic word must be Tim. As soon as his son got mentioned, she went all soft and mushy. He ought to present himself in a more fatherly fashion.

"I guess he loves sports," she murmured.

"Baseball, not football. Actually, he thinks this tie is pretty ugly, too. But I still wear it, anyway. I guess I'm a sentimental fool."

"To be sentimental about your son isn't foolish," she said.

He suppressed a triumphant smile. Tim was obviously the quickest way to her heart. He'd be wise not to tell her he owned only three ties, and she'd already seen two of them. Let her think he'd chosen the football tie only out of paternal sentiment.

The bus exited the highway, the driver steering less jaggedly, to Gary's great regret. He had no excuse to wrap his arm around Sophie, no excuse to bury his nose in her hair and brush his lips against the curls. "It's so rural here," she exclaimed as the van headed west on Route 20. "This must be like where you live."

"This," he corrected her, "is the suburbs." It didn't seem all that rural to him. For that matter, the town he lived in no longer seemed particularly rural. In the years since his childhood, Boston's urban sprawl had spread almost as far as

Stow. Housing developments and minimalls had sprouted along the main routes, and an interstate passed close to the town's limits.

"That newspaper you were reading yesterday—is this the region it reports on?"

He couldn't stifle a laugh. "You sound as if you think we've left the planet Earth for another galaxy. This is the 'burbs. We're ten minutes from the city."

"Well, I just..." She lowered her eyes. "I'm just thinking about how different your life must be."

Different from hers, was what she was thinking. Different enough that she didn't want to pursue anything with him. Even if he was a daddy in an ugly tie. Even if he'd experienced ennobling grief. His life was too different.

Well, okay. He would concede that they were from different worlds. So what? They spoke the same language. They understood each other.

The stenographer twisted in her seat to face him. "You live around here?" she asked.

He wondered how much of his and Sophie's conversation she'd overheard, then decided he really didn't care if she'd committed to memory every word they'd exchanged. "I live maybe another ten miles out, in Stow."

"What do they charge for a manicure around there? Less than in the city, I bet."

"I wouldn't know." He peeked at Sophie's hands once more. Her nails were pretty, not particularly long but polished with a pale pink gloss.

"I'm always breaking my nails. That steno machine is murder on them. Where do you get yours done?" she asked Sophie.

"In my bedroom," Sophie said. Gary swallowed a groan. He didn't care a lick about manicures, but Sophie's bedroom... He could really care about that if he let himself.

Sophie and the stenographer began to chatter about various nail salons in downtown Cambridge. Gary stayed where he was, in his mind's image of Sophie's bedroom. He pictured soft pastels, artsy things from her shop, thick pale carpeting. A broad bed covered with a puffy white comforter. Six pillows of assorted shapes. Her hair splayed out on a few of those pillows, and her body stretched across the comforter. Naked. Sweet and golden, a sculpture of swells and shadows, curves and hollows.

He placed himself in the picture and liked what he saw. It didn't matter if they were from different worlds; this was one world where they could coexist quite nicely.

Just thinking about it was enough to keep him happily occupied until they reached the chapel. The bus steered up the horseshoe-shaped brick driveway that led to an excruciatingly picturesque building. It looked like something from a Currier & Ives etching, one part white clapboard and three parts New England charm—and ten parts romance, if one happened to be of the female persuasion. All the women on the bus—including the stenographer and even the crusty gray-haired judge—let out a collective sigh as the bus drew to a halt before the pillared front porch.

"Remember, you are not to speak about anything you see," the judge admonished them all as she rose from her seat.

Sophie didn't have to speak. She spun in her seat to face Gary, and he was nearly blinded by the light in her eyes.

They shimmered, they glimmered, they all but exploded with lovey-dovey ideas about the chapel.

Well, he thought sourly, Jocelyn Kramer's certainly won a few jurors to her side of the suit. She'd won every juror who bought into the clichés of romance, every juror who thought a pretty white chapel on a pretty country road, surrounded by pretty grass and pretty trees and a pretty millstream just across the way, was all it took to make a marriage worthwhile. She'd won every juror who believed the trappings were more important than the feelings.

Judging by her radiant smile, Gary knew Sophie was one of those giddy, swooning jurors. And he wasn't the least bit pleased about it.

5

SOPHIE WANTED TO WEEP. She wasn't the type of woman who dissolved into tears for no good reason, but strolling through the lovely New England bridal chapel, and then the enchanting historic inn where the wedding dinner was to have taken place, forced her to confront how the magnificent romance of Jocelyn Kramer's wedding had been dashed to bits by a selfish bastard. It was all so heartbreakingly beautiful, so unbearably romantic. Sophie wanted to grieve for Jocelyn and every other woman who'd ever been treated like dirt by a man.

Which was just about every other woman in the world, no doubt. Certainly Sophie would qualify as a charter member of that miserable club.

Gary never left her side throughout the tour of the chapel and the inn. He didn't dare to touch her, but as the seven jurors were shuffled in and out of the chapel, across a grassy field to the inn and up the stairs to the second-floor ballroom where the dinner would have been, he was always within reach, matching his gait to hers, his attention on their surroundings but his body language speaking to her on a private line. She wondered about the wedding he'd had, about the bride he'd loved and lost. Had they hosted a formal dinner like the one Jocelyn Kramer had planned? Or had Gary and his wife been married in a down-home farm-style manner? What *was* a farm-style wedding, anyway? Something like a barn raising, perhaps, with the bride in gingham and the groom in overalls, and bales of hay for the congregation to sit on.

Ridiculous. Gary was a man of the present, and his wedding had probably been just like any other. Except that it had ended in tragedy. His wife had died, leaving him a son to raise. The thought fed Sophie's sadness.

If he was recalling his own doomed marriage, he gave no hint of it. His face remained impassive throughout the jurors' tour of the wedding site. The court officers had ordered them to keep their feelings to themselves. At least for now, Gary had decided to be a good boy and behave.

Sophie behaved, too. She remained dry-eyed and stoic as she jotted notes onto her pad. She entered a sketch of the chapel onto one page, and a description of the seating arrangements and decor of the second-floor reception room at the inn. She recorded the menu Jocelyn Kramer and her mother had selected for the wedding dinner, the flower centerpieces they had ordered. She made a note of what wines had been chosen to accompany the dinner.

Thank God her own wedding plans hadn't gotten that far. She would have loved to get married in a ceremony identical to the one Jocelyn Kramer had dreamed up. Sophie and Mitchell could have filled the quaint New England chapel with their family and friends. They could have partied half the night in the ballroom of the two-hundred-year-old inn. Her California relatives would have been enthralled by the historic setting, so unlike anything that existed on the West Coast. And Mitchell's family could trace its lineage back at least two hundred years. For all she knew, some of his ancestors might have celebrated their marriage at the very same inn.

Yet, when she closed her eyes and cut her imagination loose, she couldn't visualize Mitchell, staid and dignified, waiting at the front of the chapel for her to glide down the aisle to him, or ushering her out to the center of the ball-room's hardwood floor for their first dance as husband and wife. Instead, she saw Gary Brett at the front of the chapel, standing proudly in his jeans and football tie, his dark hair mussed and his hands leathery from physical labor. She saw Gary whisking her out onto the dance floor, thumbing his nose at protocol by holding her just a bit too close. She imag-ined Gary drawing her seductively to himself, resting his cheek against her hair and moving his tall, lean body against hers.

It was a truly frightening picture.

She couldn't begin to guess how he had insinuated himself so thoroughly into her mind. He was a farmer. A fellow ju-ror. Nothing more.

Nothing more? He was a widower, a brave survivor, a devoted father, an honorable man. His candid admission, during voir dire, that he had broken women's hearts didn't signify much—other than that he wasn't a liar. How many hearts could a farmer break, anyway? Particularly when he was a self-confessed sentimental fool.

Damn. She was falling for Gary Brett, falling hard, falling like a crystal paperweight off the top of the Prudential Tower. She was running a very serious risk of shattering on impact.

Thus it was a deliberate move on her part to change seats for the drive back to the court building. She maneuvered to sit with Henri, the congenial Haitian immigrant with the lilting accent. Throughout the trip, he told her about his arrival in Boston as a young man, about the proudest day of his life—when he became an American citizen four years ago—and about the volatile politics of his native country. Henri was truly fascinating. Even better, he wore a big, fat wedding band on his ring finger, so Sophie didn't think she'd have to worry about his putting his arm around her if the bus driver took a corner too swiftly.

The bus reached Cambridge at eleven-thirty. The jurors and court personnel were deposited outside one of the courthouse's back doors to spare them any delays at the front door's metal detectors, and they were whisked upstairs to the seventh floor on a service elevator at the rear of the building because, according to one of the uniformed guards, the front elevators were still experiencing mechanical difficulties. By the time the jurors had returned to the courtroom, it was almost noon.

If Sophie were living her normal life, she would right now be touching up her lipstick and receiving some last-minute coaching from Lynn in preparation for her lunchtime blind date with the investment counselor who owned property on Martha's Vineyard. Instead, Sophie found herself back in the jury box, her lipstick worn off long ago and a widowed farmer seated next to her, eyeing her with suspicion. "Is it my breath?" he whispered.

She glanced around, hoping someone was going to call the room to order. But lawyers, principals and onlookers were still dribbling into the room. The judge hadn't appeared yet. Sophie couldn't pretend the trial was demanding her full attention.

She sighed and turned back to Gary. Although all the chairs in the jury box were spaced evenly from each other, he seemed much too close to her. But then, if he were in the same room he would be too close. If he were on the same continent, he would be too close.

And there was nothing wrong with his breath.

"What are you talking about?" she whispered back.

"Just wondering why you didn't want to ride back to town with me."

Because I'm afraid of becoming too attached to you. Because after hearing about your wife's death and then touring the wedding chapel, I was too emotional. Because I'm the one in danger of turning into a sentimental fool. "I was curious to hear about Aristide's rise to power in Haiti," she fibbed.

"Oh, of course. Aristide's one of my heroes, too." His smile was dubious, but he patted her on the shoulder as if to convey that he forgave her for concocting such a ridiculous answer. His hand burned an imprint right through her blouse, an erotic warmth that seeped from her shoulder down into her body, making her forget all about Haiti's recent political turmoil.

"Gary..." She spoke through clenched teeth and hoped no one was eavesdropping. "We're jurors."

"Here, yes. Anywhere else we could be anyone else."

No, they couldn't. Anywhere else she would be Sophie Wallace, the city slicker, the shop owner, the once-jilted woman who hadn't yet given up on the possibility of a real romance with a man who would stick to his promises and live up to his commitments. And he was Gary Brett, the country boy, the single dad, the guy who'd broken some hearts and shunned city life and was too darned good-looking for Sophie's peace of mind.

Closing her eyes, she thought wistfully about her thwarted blind date. But just as at the chapel, she could picture only Gary, his rugged physique, his lopsided dimple, his thick, dark, hair and bedroom eyes.

The rattle and creak of chair hinges roused her from her reverie. People were pulling themselves to their feet to hail the judge's entrance. Gary touched Sophie's elbow as she hastened to stand, and his touch once again sent pulses of heat beneath her skin and deep into her body. No matter what sort of person the executive with the Vineyard vacation home might be, she couldn't believe he could have a more potent impact on her than Gary did.

She was in trouble. Big trouble

Easing her arm away from his hand, she watched the judge climb to her elevated chair. Instead of sitting, however, the judge turned to the jury and said, "We will take a one-hour recess for lunch. Follow the bailiff please." She punctuated the command with a rap of her gavel, then rotated and swept back out of the courtroom.

Lunch? Did that mean Sophie and Gary were going to race ahead of the other jurors and grab their own private table for two in the cafeteria?

Apparently not. As soon as all seven jurors were safely inside the jury room, a uniformed guard explained that since the trial had begun, they would not be allowed to mingle in the cafeteria, but would instead be having lunch sent up to the crowded little room adjacent to the courtroom. "You may order a ham sandwich, a turkey sandwich or a cheese sandwich," he announced. "As for drinks, your choices are coffee, milk or soda. Let's keep it simple."

"Does this mean we don't have to pay?" the sandhog asked eagerly.

"Does this mean we're being sequestered?" Louise sounded even more excited than the sandhog.

"You aren't being sequestered," the guard explained. "This is just to move things along. The trip to the wedding chapel took longer than expected. The judge wants to get through the plaintiff's case today. Having lunch sent up here will save some time."

Of course it would save time. The jurors wouldn't have the luxury of studying the cafeteria's offerings and making their own food choices. Instead, they would be stuck eating a sandwich. Sophie didn't want a sandwich.

"Cheese," she grumbled when the guard asked her to place her order. "And a diet cola, please."

"You aren't a vegetarian, are you?" Gary asked, once he'd requested a turkey sandwich and an ice tea. "Yesterday you ate yogurt, today cheese."

"I'm not a big fan of sandwich meat," she said, taking a seat at the table and trying not to care that Gary had immediately preempted the chair next to hers, that like at the chapel, he seemed determined to stick by her side. With their legs hidden under the table, no one could see how close his knee was to hers. Even she couldn't see it. She could only feel it, the disconcerting thrill of his nearness, the electrifying awareness of how hard and muscular his leg had felt when she'd planted her hand on him to brace herself during the drive to the chapel.

"I bet you'd like boutique meat," he teased.

She smiled. Why did his eyes have to be so luminous? Why did he have to have that confounded dimple? Why couldn't the lawyers have chosen a full panel of jurors before they'd reached Gary yesterday? Why couldn't he have managed to get himself disqualified, the way he'd said he would?

Why did she have to be turning all softheaded and softhearted over him?

He returned her smile, and that seemed to answer all her questions. Why? Because either fate or the justice system had destined it. Because it was time for her to expand her horizons, to meet men who weren't single urban professionals like her, to open herself up to other perspectives. Because Gary was delightful company and in another day or so, he would be a pleasant memory, and in a week she would forget all about him.

Until that week went by, until he faded from memory to zilch, so what if his leg was a little too close to hers? So what if his knee was separated from hers by only a molecule's width of air? So what if her body sizzled whenever she glimpsed his smile, if her brain conveniently deleted all thoughts of how she'd been hurt by a man before—and Gary had testified during voir dire that he had hurt women? It was only for now, for the trial. Whatever was going on between her and him wasn't lasting, or important, or real. She might as well just enjoy it for what it was.

Miss Prinz took her seat at the head of the table. "In the interest of efficiency," she declared, gazing from one juror to the next like a college professor making sure her seminar students were listening, "I think we ought to introduce ourselves while we eat. This may facilitate our deliberations later on. I am Margaret Prinz. I am an office manager at an accounting firm in Boston. This is my fourth experience on a jury, which is why I volunteered to serve as the foreman. Next," she urged Henri with a nod.

"Volunteered?" Gary whispered to Sophie. "She *stole* that job from me."

"No, from me," Sophie whispered back.

"Maybe a real foreman has to be bossy."

"I can be bossy," Sophie boasted, earning her a challenging grin from Gary and a scowl from Miss Prinz.

Henri announced that he was a city bus driver and shared with everyone the story he'd told Sophie, about the day he became an American citizen. Louise described herself as a retired homemaker—"All my little birdies have flown from the nest!" she twittered—who now kept busy with needlepoint and daytime television. "I saw every minute of the O.J. Simpson trial on Court-TV," she bragged. "Every single minute of it."

Next to her sat the sandhog, Jack, who regaled his fellow jurors with more information than Sophie would ever want to know about constructing highway tunnels underwater. Lunch arrived while the juror seated to Miss Prinz's left, Phillip, was talking about his career as a public school gym teacher from Billerica. "I've never been on a jury before," he grumbled, glaring pointedly at Miss Prinz, "and I hope to heaven I'll never be on one again."

"No editorializing," Miss Prinz chided. "And of course, no discussion of this trial."

"I wasn't discussing the trial. All I said was, watching kids in detention is more fun than this."

"That's editorializing."

"That's the fact, lady."

Miss Prinz pursed her lips and steered her gaze to Gary. "Next?"

Gary grinned, his eyes bright with mischief. "I'm Gary, I'm a farmer and I think editorializing is a great thing."

Miss Prinz's face grew even more pinched as she assessed his challenge. "As the foreman of this jury—"

"Forewoman," he corrected her. "And nobody picked you to be our censor, Miss Prinz."

"If you say anything in here about what we've done on the jury so far, you will jeopardize the trial."

"Sounds good to me," Gary shot back. "Then the judge could declare a mistrial and we can all go home. I don't know about the rest of you, but I've got irrigation lines to inspect."

"If you do anything to cause a mistrial," Miss Prinz warned, "I will report you."

"And will I get detention?" Gary turned to Phillip and winked.

"I think we should move on," Miss Prinz said dryly.

"I don't like her," Gary muttered to Sophie under his breath.

"No kidding," she muttered back.

"Your turn," Miss Prinz commanded, just as Sophie bit into her sandwich.

She chewed, aware of the silence and the expectant gazes of her fellow jurors as they waited for her to swallow. She chewed more vigorously, forced down the food with a swig of soda and faked a smile. "I'm Sophie, I own a boutique in Cambridge and if it weren't for this trial, I'd be on a lunch date right now."

Gary twisted around to face her, his smile quizzical, as if he suspected her of trying to send him a message.

She supposed that was exactly what she was doing. Reminding him—and herself—of the fact that she had a social life, or at least the potential for one, outside the courthouse, might make her a little less softheaded and softhearted. Softheadedness and softheartedness had cost her way too much when she'd agreed to marry Mitchell. She really had to work harder at resisting Gary, whom she didn't even know but who seemed to be able to turn her on with…well, with little more than a quizzical smile.

She smiled back at him. He upped the ante by nudging her under the table, his leg exerting slow, steady pressure on hers. Not a nudge, really, but…a rub. He was rubbing her thigh with his knee.

Her face burned and she took a long, icy sip of soda.

"Why don't you tell us about this date?" he asked, his leg still pressed to hers, his eyes glowing wickedly.

"Well, he's—" she took another quick sip to clear her throat "—he's a businessman, and he has a vacation house on Martha's Vineyard." Beyond that, she knew nothing about him. She could barely even recall his name.

"Isn't that romantic!" Louise gushed, sighing. "I just love it when young people fall in love. I'm so happy for you, Sophie."

Staring into Gary's eyes, Sophie decided she wasn't all that happy for herself. If anything was romantic, it was the way Gary's gaze stroked her nerves, the way his leg heated hers, the way his smile seemed to promise things she wanted but shouldn't have and didn't dare to name.

Her attempt to ward him off had failed. She only wished she could feel sorry about it.

WELL, ALL RIGHT—he wasn't the most diligent juror in the world. Then again, Jocelyn Kramer's waterworks testimony wasn't the most compelling drama in the world, either. She'd planned a wedding. She'd gotten stood up. End of story.

Gary was far more intrigued by the news that some fellow—an executive with a retreat on the Vineyard—had gotten stood up for lunch by Sophie. As excuses went, jury duty was more impressive than some of the turn-downs Gary had received in his life, but still...

Who was this boyfriend? How serious was the relationship? If Sophie was truly involved with a guy, why hadn't she bothered to say something yesterday, when Gary had kissed her? Not only hadn't she said anything, but she'd kissed Gary back, more enthusiastically than he'd expected. And she hadn't pushed his leg away when he'd gone up-close-and-personal with his knee under the table at lunch today, either.

Was she trying to lead Gary on or turn him away? Whenever he got mixed messages, he heeded the message he preferred. If Sophie wanted him to obey the *I'm seeing someone else, so leave me alone* message, she was going to have to communicate a little more clearly.

Right now she was communicating only with her notebook. She might as well have been taking dictation, her notes were so copious. It seemed as if she was recording every sob-choked word the Kramer woman uttered.

And there were lots of sob-choked words. One thing Jocelyn Kramer wasn't was reserved. She rambled on and on about her courtship with Ronald McGuire, detailing how he'd wooed her, how he'd made promises, how they'd planned their future together. "Was there ever any coercion on your part?" Attorney Laudrey asked her. "Did you pressure Mr. McGuire to make these promises?"

"No!" Jocelyn Kramer swore vehemently. "He was the one who raised the subject of marriage. He was the one who wanted to make it legal."

"But you didn't resist the idea, did you?"

"Of course not." She cast McGuire a hangdog look. "I loved him," she mourned, her voice quivering over the word *love.*

Gary allowed that she might deserve an Oscar—but certainly not the jury's vote. She did histrionics well, but logic was definitely not her long suit.

What on earth could Sophie be scribbling? He tried to peek discreetly over her shoulder, but he couldn't decipher her loopy scrawl. She gazed alternately at her pad and at the woman in the witness box. Her expression was even more earnest than Jocelyn Kramer's.

"Not once during the entire planning of the wedding did he let on that he had doubts," Jocelyn was saying, her voice wavering under the weight of her emotion. "He knew everything my family was doing. He was involved in the plans. He knew how many bridesmaids we were going to have in the party. He came with me to interview photographers. He was with me when we auditioned musicians. He was in on it, every step of the way. And not once did he ever say, 'Wait a minute—I'm having second thoughts.'"

"Did he know what the wedding was going to cost?" Laudrey asked.

I'll bet it wasn't going to cost as much as the legal fees for this suit, Gary thought sourly.

"Of course he knew. I discussed prices with him all the time. He seemed sympathetic about the expense."

"So you never had an inkling that Mr. McGuire was not in favor of this wedding."

"I thought we had an honest relationship. If only he'd told me somewhere along the way that he didn't want to marry me, I could have handled it. I would have been heartbroken, but it would have been better than leaving me at the altar on my wedding day."

"Thank you. Your witness," he said to the other lawyer, Harrison.

Vying with Laudrey for the best-tailored-lawyer award, Harrison marched up to the witness stand and eyed Jocelyn like a father determined to accept no nonsense from a daughter who'd disobeyed a rule. "You would have been heartbroken," he echoed her words.

"Of course. I loved Ronald."

"And you're heartbroken still, aren't you?"

"I don't fall in and out of love as easily as some people," she said, firing a recriminating glare at her ex-fiancé.

"So you want revenge for the pain he's caused you, is that right?"

"Objection!" Laudrey hollered, springing to his feet with the speed of an NBA forward.

"Goes to motive, Your Honor," Harrison addressed the judge.

"Overruled. You may answer the question, Ms. Kramer."

"I don't want revenge," she said, sounding suspiciously well rehearsed. "What would be the point in that? I hate

Ronald. I want him out of my life. Revenge would only prolong my connection to him." She didn't sound the least bit lachrymose anymore. Her voice was steel hard, her eyes as dry as October leaves. "All I want is reimbursement for my expenses, plus pain and suffering."

"Pain and suffering sounds a lot like revenge to me."

"It sounds a lot like pain and suffering to me," she retorted.

All right. Gary would give her half a point. He had no patience for sniveling and self-pity. But he admired toughness, and faced with the opposition, Jocelyn had turned tough.

Sophie flipped her pad to a clean page and resumed her note taking, her fingers a graceful blur as she covered the lined paper with her script. Harrison grilled Jocelyn Kramer on the wedding arrangement, getting her to admit that staging the wedding at that chapel and inn had been her idea, not McGuire's, and that money had been no object as they'd signed contracts and ordered bridal apparel. By the time Harrison was done cross-examining her, Gary was left with the clear impression that Jocelyn Kramer had been more interested in the wedding than in the groom.

That was the way it was with weddings, though: heavy-duty ceremony, oppressive ritual, but not much regard for the relationship itself. Some people focused on the wedding, and others focused on the marriage. A real marriage, a true marriage—a bond like what he'd had with Meg—wasn't about picture-postcard chapels and elaborate dinner menus. It was about a man, a woman and a promise. Period.

Harrison finished his cross-examination, ending the plaintiff's side of the case, at around four o'clock. The judge addressed the jurors. "Tomorrow," she said, "we will hear the defendant's presentation. And again, I caution you not to discuss this trial with anyone. Court will readjourn tomorrow at 9:00 a.m. We are in recess." She hammered her gavel, stood and departed from the courtroom.

"Free at last," Gary murmured under his breath.

Sophie folded her notepad shut and flexed her fingers. She frowned at him. "This isn't a joke, you know."

"You could have fooled me."

"We'd better not talk about it." She hushed him, shooting a quick, anxious look in Miss Prinz's direction.

"Okay," he said. "Let's talk about your boyfriend, instead."

Predictably, her cheeks grew beautifully rosy. "Let's not," she said, motioning with her head for him to turn around and exit the jury box.

He followed the sandhog through the narrow aisle to the end of the jury box, and then through the door out of the courtroom. In the jury room, the other jurors were collecting their jackets and sweaters and bidding each other farewell for the day.

"Why shouldn't we talk about your boyfriend?" Gary persisted, in part because he wanted to know but mostly because it was so much fun to watch Sophie blush.

She chose to ignore him. "So long, Gary," she said with false cheer. "See you tomorrow." Sliding the strap of her purse over her shoulder, she stalked out of the room.

His curiosity piqued, he chased her down the hall to the elevators. He wasn't surprised to find a huge crowd waiting in front of one set of doors. The other elevators were apparently still out of order.

"You're the one who brought up the subject," he persevered once he'd caught up with her.

"When?"

"At lunch. You said you could have been on a lunch date today."

"That doesn't mean I have a boyfriend." Her voice was as gritty as Jocelyn's had been during cross-examination.

Gary paused to take stock. Women mystified him. Even Meg, whom he'd known better than any other woman, had always been an enigma to him—and he hardly knew Sophie at all. So why would she have mentioned the lunch date if she *didn't* have a boyfriend, or if she didn't expect Gary to question her about it? Why, if she was trying to put him off, didn't she just come right out and say so?

An elevator door behind them slid open. "Is that one working?" a woman in the crowd asked.

"I don't think so," someone cautioned.

"It looks like it's working to me," Gary said, taking Sophie's arm and ushering her into the car.

A few of the people waiting in the hall murmured in confusion. "It wasn't working a few minutes ago," someone else remarked.

"Maybe it's broken," Sophie said. Abruptly the doors slid shut.

Gary shook his head confidently and pressed the ground floor button. "Okay," he said, pleased that they'd managed to snare their own private ride downstairs. "Tell me why you went public with the news that you were missing a lunch date with a rich dude."

Her fingers fluttered nervously at her sides. Her gaze

darted around the dimly lit car, finally focusing on the floor. "I don't know what to do about you, Gary."

He caught his breath and smiled. Sophie Wallace could go from perplexing to frank in ten seconds flat. "Why do you think you have to do anything about me?" he asked.

"Oh, you know." She blushed furiously.

"No, I don't."

She sighed, impatient but evidently convinced that he had no idea what she was talking about—even if he had a perfectly clear idea. He wanted to hear it in her words. "There's this—this—*thing* going on between us, and I don't know what to do about it."

Her ambivalence was appealing. Her willingness to acknowledge the *thing* blossoming between them was even more appealing. The elevator cables squeaked above them and she glanced up and winced. "What do you want to do about it?"

She lifted her eyes to him. "I'm not in the market to get hurt, okay?"

"Who says you're going to get hurt?"

"I've been hurt before," she reminded him. "I said so during voir dire."

"Everyone's been hurt before," he argued.

"We have nothing in common. You're not my type."

"What's your type? Some rich guy with a Vineyard house, whom you just invented to scare me off?"

"I didn't invent him," she argued. "I really did have a blind date set up for today."

"A blind date? You don't even know this guy?" Gary laughed. "How do you know he's your type?"

"He's..." She shrugged and then flinched when the cables

above the car gave another ominous squeak. "I have no idea if he's my type, either. This isn't about him. It's about you."

"Me, or my ugly tie?"

She wrestled with a smile. "You're a family man. You're settled in the country, with your dogs and your apple trees. That's not what I'm looking for."

"You're looking for some rich guy you don't even know?"

"If you really must know, I'm looking for someone I can build a solid future with," she told him.

A future? Whoa! Who was talking about a future? "We kissed, Sophie. We kissed, and I happen to be of the opinion that we ought to do it again. I'm not looking any further into the future than that."

"Well, then, that's another difference between you and me. I *am* looking into the future. I'm a lot more careful than you are about this kind of thing."

"This kind of *thing*, you mean?" he emphasized. Her hair tempted him. Her hair, so lush and luxurious and downright gorgeous, was part of the *thing*. And if he didn't touch it right away, the elevator was going to arrive in the courthouse lobby and he would have to convince her to accept a ride home from him if he hoped to have another minute alone with her.

He reached out and ran his index finger along one shiny tress. The curl spiraled around his finger and he suppressed a groan. Her hair was soft and silky and incredibly sexy.

"Gary." Her voice sounded as soft and silky as her hair felt. She pulled back from him and drew in a shaky breath.

"You want me as much as I want you," he murmured.

"I don't want any of this." She sounded exasperated and more than a bit panicked.

"But you can't help yourself," he guessed.

"It's just plain wrong. We've got a commitment to the legal system—"

"What are we doing that could harm our commitment? Which part of it is wrong?"

"We're supposed to be objective."

"About the trial. Not about each other."

"I can't..." She closed her eyes and sucked in another shaky breath. "I can't think when you look at me like that. And I have to be able to think, Gary. I want to get through this jury duty without going crazy. Okay? Can you understand that?"

If he didn't kiss her, *he'd* go crazy. "Let's assume the trial is going to end tomorrow. Safe assumption, right?"

She studied him as if she suspected him of setting her up.

"Safe assumption," he answered himself. "So, after the trial, would it be all right for me to kiss you?"

"I don't know. No." She sighed, and stared at the sealed elevator doors. "I just don't think we're a good match."

"We're more flammable than any match, and you know it."

"I'd rather not know it," she confessed, once again startling him with her candor.

"Sophie," he murmured, reaching out to her again.

And then the elevator lurched to a halt and went pitch-black. Screaming, she tumbled into his arms.

6

AFTER THE FIRST SHOCK, she wasn't alarmed. Elevators—even unlit, broken elevators—didn't frighten her.

Yet Gary's arms felt so good around her, she didn't want to back off quite yet and reassure him that she was fine. She wasn't going to pretend she was frightened, but really, where was the harm in letting him console her for just a few precious seconds more? No matter that her feelings about him were mixed; *these* feelings weren't mixed at all. *These* feelings informed her quite clearly that being held by Gary Brett was a divine experience.

His arms were strong—not bulging with unnecessary muscle the way a weight lifter's might be, but strong from genuine labor. From lifting and hauling and fixing things, bringing plants to life and making them grow, raising crops, raising a son. His arms possessed the kind of strength a man needed to support a grief-stricken young child when the most important woman in their lives was gone.

Comforting strength, that was it. Soothing, warming, intimate strength. Strength that derived not from brawn but from the heart, from the soul.

He smelled clean and male. In the close, dark elevator car, she became acutely aware of traits not apparent to the eye—the sleek contours of his chest, the minty scent of his aftershave, the cheap polyester texture of his football necktie. She heard the constant rhythm of his breath. She sensed the so-lidity of him, the unshakable confidence. This was a man a woman could lean on, if she had to. This was a man who be-lieved in being honest.

"There's probably an emergency button somewhere," he murmured, making no move to loosen his embrace. "We should be able to signal for someone to rescue us."

The only thing Sophie needed to be rescued from was her own treacherous yearnings. Being trapped in a stalled, light-less elevator was nowhere near as dangerous as being trapped within Gary's arms—not because he refused her the chance to escape but because she refused herself the chance. Why waste this opportunity? As long as they were stuck in the broken elevator, unable to do anything else, why not make the most of it?

Which was really a very bad way to think about the situa-tion.

Gary must have been thinking the same bad way. He slid one hand slowly up her back and under her hair to the nape of her neck. By the time she felt his fingertips against her skin, their gentle friction unleashing a flood of warmth through her body, her eyes had adjusted enough to the dark to make out his tall, rugged silhouette looming before her.

Her imagination filled in what her eyes couldn't see. She knew he would be smiling; she knew his dimple would be denting his left cheek. She knew his eyes would be luminous, chips of emerald imbedded in silver and gold. She knew his hair would be tousled. She knew his mouth would be wait-ing for hers, hungry for hers.

She tilted her head up as he tilted his down. In the instant before their lips met, she was convinced that she could see him, all of him—the longing in his gaze, the energy that powered his body, his innate honesty and his ability to break a woman's heart. She could see opportunity and risk, safety and peril. If not with her eyes, she could see it with her soul.

And then her vision was obliterated by heat and darkness, by his kiss.

It was nothing like yesterday's hesitant, experimental kiss in his car. This kiss was hot-blooded, full throttled, the kind of kiss a man gave a woman when nothing was stopping him.

She moaned as his mouth moved against hers. The heat of his kiss burned down her throat and into her breasts, her hips, her knees, her toes. Her entire body seemed to glow like hot embers about to burst into flame.

She felt simultaneously weak and omnipotent. She felt possessive and possessed. She felt as if she were soaring, even as she was sinking deeper and deeper into the lush passion of Gary's kiss. She felt as if she could carry the world on her back, even though her legs were barely steady enough to hold her upright.

She reached up and grabbed hold of him, arching her fingers around his shoulders. Through his blazer she could feel hard ridges of sinew and bone, the fine, taut sculpture of his torso. His hands clenched, one sliding up into the heavy mass of her hair and the other moving against the small of her back. They felt so large, one of them cupping her head and holding it steady, the other nearly spanning her waist. His breath caught on something low and rough in his throat, and then he parted her lips with his tongue.

He tasted as good as he felt, strong and intoxicating. His tongue touched hers, tangled with it, lunged and parried and conquered. She sighed with pleasure and frustration, grateful for what she had, yet wanting more—and feeling greedy for wanting. When she moved against him his breath caught again, and he brought his hand lower, molding his palm to the curve of her bottom and guiding her hips against his.

He murmured something. She wasn't sure of the exact words. Something about how aroused he was, something about how much he wanted her, something about taking her right there, in the darkness, if she would let him.

She murmured something back, just as unintelligible. Probably enthusiastic agreement.

He skimmed his hand over her hip and up along her ribs to her breast. She arched into him, delighting in his touch, in the way the pressure of his hand on her awakened other pressures deep inside her. He brought his other hand forward, down to her other breast, and rubbed his thumbs over her nipples. She shuddered with pleasure.

He whispered her name. She heard him clearly this time, heard the roundness of the first syllable, the anguished groan of the second. "Sophie... Oh, you feel so good."

"Yes."

"So sweet..."

"Yes."

"I'm burning up... Sophie..."

"I know, I know." She brought her hands forward and loosened his tie, an act of mercy for this overheated man. No, not mercy—mere selfishness. She fumbled with his collar button, felt it give and then decided that opening any more buttons would require too much effort. Instead, she skimmed her hands down his chest to his belt. By the time her fingers had alighted on the buckle, he was wrestling with the buttons of her skirt. He plucked open two of them, then reached inside the slit and stroked upward, sliding between her thighs.

His hand was hot. Her entire body was hot. She couldn't deal with his belt. She couldn't deal with anything but the feel of his palm cupping her, his fingers stroking her through her pantyhose, so hot against her, so very hot.

"Hello?"

The voice echoed from somewhere miles—or at least a few floors—above them. Gary's hand continued to move against her, a little less insistently, as if he wanted to bring them both down gradually. He let out a ragged breath and eased his hand out from under her skirt, then smoothed the fabric over her hips.

"Anyone down there?" the nasal tenor resounded in the elevator shaft.

"Damn," Gary muttered, his breathing still uneven. "I need a minute."

Sophie swallowed, not trusting her voice.

"Hello?" their unwelcome rescuer hollered down to them. "Can you hear me?"

Gary directed his voice toward the ceiling. "Yeah, we can hear you!"

"How many people are stuck in there?"

"Two."

"Have you got any power at all?"

"Enough to light up the city," Gary murmured, brushing his hand gently against Sophie's cheek and then grazing her brow with a light, tender kiss. "No power!" he shouted.

"Okay! Just sit tight! Don't panic! We'll get you out of there!"

"Who's panicked?" Gary asked Sophie.

She could picture his smile. She could feel its warmth radiating through the darkness. But as reality slowly stole over her, she admitted that she *should* be panicked.

Just minutes ago she had been explaining that she was confused and troubled by her feelings for him. That ambivalence hadn't changed. The only thing that had changed was that she'd discovered an enormous, hitherto-untapped reserve of lust inside her.

Not just lust. Lust for Gary Brett.

"I guess we've learned our lesson," he said, at last stepping backward and giving her some space. She sagged against the wall, her strength draining from her, and let out a long sigh.

"What lesson?" she asked in an uncharacteristically husky tone.

"Never take a chance on an unreliable elevator."

That was hardly the most important lesson she'd learned. Actually, everything else she'd learned in the last couple of minutes sat in a jumbled pile in her brain, in desperate need of sorting. But as long as she was trapped with Gary—hearing his sexy voice, inhaling his sexy scent and remembering the demoralizingly sexy feel of his hands on her, his body against her—she wasn't going to be able to sort anything out.

"I meant what I said before," she warned him.

"Which part? About our commitment to the American legal system?"

"About our being a bad match."

He threw back his head and laughed. His laughter waned

at the ominous sound of cables creaking overhead, but she heard amusement in his voice when he spoke again. "Who needs matches when we've got spontaneous combustion working for us?"

All right. She was finally beginning to panic. The further she distanced herself from their mad sexual spree of a few minutes ago, the more she realized what a mistake it had been. "You don't know anything about me, Gary—"

"I know plenty about you. You're a big-city girl. You think men are scum, but you sure as hell like kissing them."

"I am not loose," she snapped, hoping her anger would conceal her defensiveness. "I'm not the kind of woman who makes out with strangers in elevators."

"We aren't strangers," he insisted, sounding far too reasonable for her peace of mind.

"We don't know each other well. We only just met. I like to know a man pretty well before I'll even consider getting involved with him."

"The American legal system—to which we are committed—has managed to get us involved with each other."

"Not the way we were involved when we...just now, when we..." Feeling her cheeks burn, she inhaled and turned from him. She resented the fact that merely by thinking about the way they'd been involved a minute ago reignited the still-smoldering heat between her legs and made her hate whoever had shouted down the shaft to them. "I'm thirty years old," she said, forcing her voice to remain level. "I'm not looking to fool around with passing strangers. That is not my idea of a good time."

"What's your idea of a good time?"

Why did he have to keep interrogating her? She was too

frazzled to have this discussion. A metallic clang overhead gave her an excuse not to answer.

Not a good enough excuse. "You seemed to be having a good time until you thought about it," he observed.

"Yes, and now I'm thinking about it."

"So am I. I'm thinking you're smart, and funny, and beautiful, and when we kiss, it's pretty damned spectacular. I'm thinking that being stuck in here with you has definitely been one of the highlights of my life."

"I don't want to be a highlight of your life," she said sharply. "For heaven's sake, that makes me sound like part of the eleven o'clock sports report on TV. 'And now, for the game highlights.'"

He laughed again, a low, throaty chuckle. "Sophie Wallace scored a knock-out, flattening Gary Brett in one round."

She didn't want to laugh, but she couldn't seem to help herself. "Flattening you?"

"Well, okay, certain parts of me weren't flattened."

She blushed, thinking about precisely which part of him hadn't been flattened. Actually, it seemed to her that she'd been the one KO'd in this bout. She still felt a bit punch-drunk.

"I'll tell you what," he said, and then the lights flickered on and off and on again.

Sophie squinted. Once her eyes had adjusted, she turned her gaze to the man sharing the elevator with her. His appearance startled her. His hair was tousled—by her fingers; his collar lay undone—by her hand; his shirt was wrinkled and bagging out where she had clawed at his belt buckle. She didn't dare to look any lower than his belt. He must have recovered by now, but she didn't even want to risk a glimpse down there.

If he looked so disheveled, no doubt she did, too. She noticed the gap where her skirt buttons were undone, and she hastily fastened them. Glancing back up, she saw that he was watching her intently.

"You're even sexier in the light than you are in the dark," he murmured. He was smiling, but his eyes were solemn.

It hurt to look at him. She hated blushing, and she knew his words had set fire to her cheeks, just as his hands had set fire to her body. It also hurt because he was impossibly sexy in the light, in the dark and every which way. "You were going to tell me something," she mumbled, gazing resolutely at the brown wall panels behind him.

"I think I just did." Then he laughed quietly, as if to reassure her. "Actually, I was going to ask if you were free this evening."

"I'm not going on a date with you."

"Gee. Think about it, take your time."

The elevator trembled, ascended perhaps a foot and then stalled again. At least the light remained on. "I thought we'd decided that we weren't going to—to do anything about this—this—" she gave up on finding a tasteful euphemism for the erotic fever that afflicted them "—until after the trial."

"But then the lights went out and everything changed." He moved closer to her, one step and then another. She had no room to back away, so she mustered her courage and held her ground. "I'm not talking about a date, Sophie. I've got to go home and check in on Tim. I was figuring you could come back to Stow with me for dinner. That's all."

"Dinner with you and your son?" That sounded even more serious than a date.

"And my father, and my two beloved but mentally deficient dogs."

"Your dogs," she echoed, truly gripped by panic now. This was it—the works, the big guns, the Seventh Cavalry. Gary wasn't going to seduce her with his passionate kisses and his talented hands. He was going to seduce her with his *family*.

"I don't know," she hedged, appalled at how tempted she was to say yes. "I really should put some time in at the store."

"When does the store close?"

"On Tuesdays? Six o'clock."

He made a big show of reading his watch. She glanced at hers, too. It was already after five. She knew what he was going to say before he said it. "There doesn't seem to be much point in that. By the time we get out of here, it could be six already."

"Well...but..." She groped for an excuse, any reason to say no, other than the truth. She was afraid that if she had dinner with him and his kid and his dad and his mentally deficient dogs on the farm, she might actually *like* it. "How would I get there?"

"I'd drive you, of course."

"Then how would I get home?"

"I'd drive you home."

"That's a lot of driving."

"You're right. Forget I asked." He laughed.

"Well...but if you drove me home, I wouldn't ask you in. I mean, you're not going to spend the night at my place."

"Oh. In that case, *definitely* forget I asked." He touched her elbow, then slid his hand up her arm to her shoulder and clasped it lightly, gently. "I'm asking you to have dinner at my house, with some nosy chaperones. There's no hidden agenda here. You think we're strangers, and maybe you're right. So let's stop being strangers. Come on over and chow down."

"All right," she heard herself say. "If we ever get out of here, I'll come."

His grin imbued his face with energy, dimpling his cheek. He craned his neck to peer up at the ceiling and bellowed, "Get us out of here! Now!"

Sophie wasn't sure whether getting out of the broken elevator would be her salvation or her doom. But she smiled anyway.

"ALL RIGHT NOW," Pop said. "Tell me the truth. Who is she?"

Gary chopped one final stalk of celery into small pieces and tossed them into the salad bowl. He and Sophie had arrived at the house less than ten minutes ago, and his father had immediately put him to work in the kitchen so they could get dinner cooked and on the table—although Gary suspected that his father had really put him to work in the kitchen so he could grill him about Sophie.

He had phoned ahead from Sophie's apartment to give Pop some warning that he had invited a friend to join the family for dinner. They'd stopped at her place because she wanted to change into more comfortable, casual clothing.

He'd been glad Sophie wanted to change. It would make her fit in better. Her idea of casual turned out to be a pair of nicely tailored wool trousers and a silky-looking shirt.

She'd seemed somewhat nervous about inviting him in to her apartment, but he'd pointed out that he wanted to phone his father and son to tell them to set another place at the table, and if he didn't phone from her place they would have to stop at a gas station along the way so he could use a pay phone. She'd admitted that that seemed foolish, so she'd let him come inside with her.

Her apartment was pretty much what he'd imagined: small but decorated to the hilt, not just with such oddities as furniture that matched and rugs that shared a color scheme with the curtains, but also with assorted elegant-looking doodads that he assumed came from her shop. Shelves held hand-blown glass vases, ceramic plates and carved-wood objets d'art resembling no known articles from the planet Earth. A tapestry hung on one wall; a stained-glass rendering of a star and a crescent moon dangled from a thread in front of one window. Needlepoint pillows were strewn about with abandon, making Gary think of Sophie behind the closed bedroom door, strewn across her bed with abandon but without her skirt and blouse.

He'd had to prove himself trustworthy, so he'd shunted the image from his mind and entered her closet-size kitchen, where she had told him he would find a phone. He'd dialed, Tim had answered and Gary had apologized for being late— "Believe it or not, I got stuck in a broken elevator with another juror," he'd reported—and announced that he was bringing the juror home for dinner. "You get stuck in an elevator with someone long enough, and you become friends."

"No problem," Tim had assured him. "We can feed your friend. Grampa's making spaghetti." Not the gourmet cui-

sine Gary could have offered Sophie if they'd gone to a restaurant, but he'd get around to taking her to a restaurant
some other night.

Sophie seemed to be handling the situation well enough.
She was seated with Tim in the front parlor of the old farmhouse, and the dogs had gathered around her feet and were
gazing up at her with goofy, smitten smiles. Gary had been
granted all of thirty seconds to remove his tie and jacket, and
now he was performing KP for his father, who seemed far
too curious about the dinner guest.

"I told you, Pop," Gary said, assessing the salad bowl's
contents and deciding another stalk of celery was required.
"She's a friend."

"She doesn't look like a friend."

"Oh?" He chopped the celery, his knife blade making stac-
cato clicks against the wood cutting board. "What does a
friend look like?"

"A friend looks like someone you'd find standing at the
urinal next to yours in a public rest room," said Pop.

Gary glanced sideways at his father, who was adding ad-
ditional herbs and spices to the spaghetti sauce he'd emptied
from a jar into a pot. Alton Brett wore his sixty-six years well.
He stood tall, he had little fat on his skeleton, and anyone
who saw him could guess where Gary's stubborn chin and
lopsided dimple came from. Alton was widowed like his
son, but unlike him, Alton had a steady sweetheart, a divor-
cée from Concord with whom he spent every Saturday night
but not much more than that. He and she feared that if they
spent more than one night a week together they'd wind up
despising each other.

The arrangement worked for them. Alton had had a drearily passionless marriage with Gary's mother, and when she'd died, he had vowed never to marry again. Gary had learned early on, by witnessing his parents' chilly relationship up close, that a marriage didn't guarantee love.

On the other hand, Alton often made loud noises about how Gary should find a mother for his son. He made even louder noises whenever Gary brought a woman to the house. No one Gary had ever dated was good enough to raise Tim, Alton believed. None of the women Gary had dated deserved the privilege of becoming a stepmother to the most remarkable grandson the world had ever known. Gary had never seriously considered any of them stepmother material, but that didn't matter. His father rejected them all anyway.

Gary hoped that, as long as his father saw Sophie as nothing more than Gary's friend, she might not be condemned out of hand. The truth was, she might wind up being nothing more than a friend. That glorious interlude in the broken elevator might be as close as Gary ever came to becoming her lover. She'd enjoyed it as much as he did—she was honest enough not to deny that—but she'd also told him she was confused and unsure.

There was nothing confused or unsure about the way she kissed. Nothing ambivalent about the way she responded when he touched her.

He scraped the chunks of celery from the cutting board into the bowl and carried it into the dining room. As he placed it on the table, he spied on Sophie and Tim in the parlor. Sophie was seated on the couch, her feet buried under the dogs. Tim lounged in Gary's favorite easy chair, his size-eleven sneakers propped on the ottoman and his flannel shirt hanging open to reveal a T-shirt emblazoned with the words Get Naked And Party across his chest.

Where the hell had that shirt come from?

If it offended Sophie, she wasn't letting on. She was talking amiably enough with Tim. Inching closer to the arched doorway leading from the dining room to the parlor, Gary eavesdropped.

"But what if you deliberately stepped into the path of the ball? Then you would automatically get to go to first. That doesn't seem fair."

"Yeah, well, but that would be like a really lame thing to do. A pitch is coming at you, like, sixty miles an hour. It hits you wrong, you're in a cast for six weeks, if not worse. It's, like, orthopedist city. Plus the ump'll call you on it. What?" he asked in a different tone of voice.

Sophie looked bewildered. "What do you mean, what?"

"You look bummed."

"No, I—" her voice was as light and musical as crystal wind chimes. "It's just that I think my foot's gone numb."

"Kick the dog. He'll move."

Gary watched as she nudged Plato with her foot. Plato gazed up at her, panting exuberantly.

"They're great dogs," Tim said. "Stupid, but great."

"Why are they named Plato and Socrates if they're stupid?"

"I don't know. My dad has a weird sense of humor."

Thanks a heap, Gary thought, returning to the kitchen to open a bottle of wine. *Get Naked And Party?* Jeez!

He worked the cork out of a bottle of Italian red table wine and turned in time to witness his father flinging a strand of spaghetti against the wall. "You know, Pop, there are better ways of testing whether spaghetti is cooked."

Alton peeled the limp strand of pasta from the wallpaper and threw it into the sink. "I do things my own way. How's your friend doing? Has Tim driven her crazy yet?"

"I don't even think he's trying."

"What are they talking about?"

Gary sighed. "She thinks the dogs are stupid."

This met with Alton's approval. "I like her," he announced.

Five minutes later, they were gathered around the table in the small dining room. Like the parlor, it was furnished with old, heavy pieces—a mahogany chest and hutch built sturdier than a bunker, the shelves displaying mismatched Depression glass that Gary's mother used to collect, beer mugs with a variety of tavern names etched into them, ashtrays from assorted motels, and a pair of tarnished silver candlesticks.

Sophie sat across the table from him. His father occupied the head of the table, and Tim flopped onto a chair at the opposite end. Alton eyed Sophie speculatively, then said, "We like to say grace before we eat."

Sophie sent him a dazzling smile. It took a minute for Alton to recover his wits and bow his head. "Lord, we give thanks for the food on this table, and for our health, and for all the good things in our lives. Thank you for making the spaghetti stick to the wall, and thank you for a full day without sass from Tim, and if you have the chance, could you please shorten this dang trial of Gary's because we really could use him helping us get the irrigation system tuned up for the season. Amen."

Sophie mouthed an "amen" with Gary and Tim, but her gaze was quizzical as it met Gary's. "Spaghetti on the wall?"

"Don't ask," Gary murmured. "The stuff in the bowl wasn't on the wall. Help yourself."

She took a small portion, then passed the bowl to Tim, who unapologetically took half of what was left. The salad and bread were passed, the wine poured. Gary asked Tim how his day at school was. "Sass-free, I take it?"

"Oh, I did lots of sassing in school. Grampa was just talking about at home."

Wise ass, Gary thought. A quick glimpse at Sophie informed him that she found Tim amusing.

"So, what about this trial?" Alton asked.

"We can't discuss it, Pop. Not even with each other," Gary said, exchanging another gaze with Sophie.

"That's so lame," Tim complained. "It's like, you're living it, but you can't talk about it."

"After the trial is done, I'll tell you all about it."

"Is it like O.J. on Court-TV?"

"No, Tim. It's a civil trial, not a criminal trial."

Tim rolled his eyes. "Listen to this. You sound like an expert."

"Spend a day and a half on a jury, and you learn. Isn't that right, Sophie?"

"It's been quite a learning experience," she agreed, smiling enigmatically.

God, she was beautiful. And seductive. He could easily become obsessed with her.

"So what happened in the elevator?" Tim asked innocently.

"Nothing!" Sophie and Gary answered in unison. Their

eyes met above the salad bowl, and her cheeks blossomed pink. Gary felt all the blood in his body rush to his groin.

"Well, the elevator broke, didn't it? Were you, like, dangling by a thread?"

"No," Gary said.

Sophie laughed, just a hint of tension in her smile. "It *was* scary," she explained to Tim. "I'd rather not think about it."

Gary hoped she was only trying to deflect Tim's questions. He himself had no intention of forgetting what happened in the elevator.

"My friend Jason went to Walt Disney World. They've got this ride where you plunge fifteen stories in an elevator."

"I think I'd faint," Sophie said, her cheeks losing color as she contemplated the possibility.

"I'd revive you," Gary assured her. Her cheeks darkened again. They were like a barometer of her emotions. The rosier the blush, the more Gary knew she was thinking about him, about them, about the way they spontaneously combusted when the conditions were just so. Being a considerate host, he directed his attention back to Tim, giving her a chance to compose herself. "So what, besides not sassing anyone, did you do in school today?" he asked his son.

Tim managed to carry the rest of the dinner conversation. He entertained Sophie with descriptions of his social studies teacher, who was definitely a direct descendant of Cruella DeVille, and his math teacher who was way cool, and his baseball team, and this idiot kid who got suspended for bringing a Swiss Army knife to school. Sophie politely listened to his long-winded tales. If she was bored, she hid her boredom well.

"Tim and I'll clean up," Alton said, once Tim had consumed every last edible substance on the table. "Why don't you and Sophie go settle on the porch and finish that bottle of wine?" This was a sign that Alton was infatuated with Sophie. If he didn't think she was terrific, he would have maneuvered to have Gary do the dishes so Gary couldn't go off somewhere with her.

"No more wine for me," Sophie said, setting her glass firmly away from herself.

"Why don't we take the dogs for a walk and I can show you around?" Gary suggested. She might be wearing tailored trousers, but her shoes were well-made loafers. She could handle the gentle hills and rutted dirt roads of the farm.

"I'd love that," she said. "As long as the dogs don't step on my feet and crush a few bones." She rose from her chair as Gary did, and smiled at him.

Just like his father, he all but melted in the glow of her smile. Except that melting implied softening, and Gary knew that if he and Sophie took an evening stroll into the orchard, he was going to kiss her again, kiss her the way he'd kissed her in the elevator, kiss her until she was no longer confused and unsure.

And if he kissed her that way, softening would not come close to describing what she did to him.

Which, of course, was just fine with him.

_____ **7** _____

LONG INTO THE NIGHT, Sophie lay awake, thinking, remembering, wondering. Wondering why hiking between two
rows of gnarled apple trees, their gray branches dotted with
tiny new leaves, and listening as Gary explained the differ-
ences between Cortlands and Macs, had seemed so interesting. Wondering why those two lumbering, bumbling dogs
had appealed to her so much. Wondering why the stillness of
the orchard hadn't spooked her, why the sweet-scented air
had soothed her, why Gary's kiss as they'd stood in the acreage behind his house had been only the most marvelous
thing in an evening of marvels.

Charming a man's family had never been one of Sophie's
talents. Mitchell had loved her—or so he'd claimed—and
asked her to marry him, and she'd moved all the way across
the country to be with him...and then she'd met his family.
To this day, she still wasn't sure what she'd done wrong,
other than to be herself. Mitchell's parents had taken one
look at her, with her wild hair, her uncensored opinions and
her arty interests, and they'd decided that she simply would
not do. The last Sophie had heard of Mitchell had been a
wedding announcement in the *Boston Globe*, less than a year
after he'd ended their engagement. According to the announcement, he had married a nice young lady whose middle name was Adams or Winthrop or something equally

*Mayflower*ish, whose father owned an investment firm and whose mother sat on the boards of three-quarters of the city's cultural foundations, and who was known to her friends as Buffy. The wedding had taken place at the Ritz-Carlton, and everyone who was anyone in the greater Boston area had been invited.

Obviously Sophie wasn't anyone. Not that she would have attended if she *had* been invited, of course.

Then there had been her boyfriend in high school. His mother had despised Sophie, probably because his father had always flirted with her, a situation which made her reluctant to visit her boyfriend's house, which in turn made his parents dislike her even more. In college, she'd had the misfortune to meet the parents of a fellow she was going out with. While visiting the campus, his mother had insisted on taking Sophie shopping, because she had four sons and no daughters and had spent her entire life longing to buy clothing for a girl. Unfortunately, her taste in apparel ran to floral fabrics and ruffles—the sort of party dresses little girls were supposed to wear with patent-leather Mary Janes. When Sophie had suggested that such fashions were not her style, the woman had never forgiven her.

Her varied experiences had proven to her that she simply didn't make a good impression on the families of men she might be interested in.

Gary's father had seemed to like her, though. Even more amazing, Gary's son had seemed to like her. Most amazing of all, she'd liked Gary's father and son. Sophie Wallace, the city mouse, had been almost as enraptured by the farm and the farm family as she'd been by the farmer.

Almost.

The kiss in the orchard hadn't been quite as steamy as the kiss in the broken elevator. Gary's hands hadn't strayed from her shoulders, and hers had remained tucked gently against his chest. Yet she'd felt the fierce drumbeat of his heart when their lips had met.

"I can't," she'd protested after a moment, pulling her mouth from his and resting her head on his shoulder.

"No one can see us here," he'd whispered. "Except for the dogs, and they don't count. They're too stupid."

"It's not your family," she'd explained. "It's the trial, Gary. I just—I think we ought to cool it until the trial is over."

"And once the trial is over?"

She had gazed up at him. The sun had set, but a faint mauve light had lingered in the air, washing the strong planes and angles of his face, the sharp dot of his dimple, his eyes. "Once the trial is over," she'd said, "we'll see."

"We'll do more than see," he'd promised, releasing her.

They'd returned to the house. Gary had checked to make sure Tim was tackling his homework, and then he'd driven Sophie back to Cambridge. The half-hour trip had been as silent as their first brief drive in his Saab, but this time the silence had been companionable, not pulsing with tension.

Or, more accurately, the tension this time had been one of anticipation, one of knowing that in a day—maybe less—they would do more than seeing, or kissing.

Still, there was that final day of the trial, and she desperately needed to empty her mind of everything but Jocelyn Kramer's suit against Ronald McGuire. "Breach of contract" seemed too sterile a phrase for what McGuire had done to the poor woman. Sophie had recovered from her own bro-

ken engagement, but she was tough—and she hadn't even
begun to look at wedding venues, let alone bought a dress,
gathered bridesmaids, booked a band and sent out engraved
invitations.

She assumed the judge was going to place limits on what
the jury could award Jocelyn. But if it were up to Sophie,
she'd award the plaintiff a million dollars, and maybe a certain part of McGuire's anatomy, severed from his body and
dipped in bronze.

And then, once revenge had been exacted through the legal system, she could do more than see with Gary Brett.

SHE HAD ON A WHITE BLOUSE, sleek black slacks and a jacket
constructed of a woven fabric with vibrant stripes of red, yel-
low, green and black. The sleeves were wide bells, cuffed at
her wrists, and instead of buttons the jacket had tie strings
adorned with black beads. No doubt it was extremely fash-
onable. Tim would probably call it wicked awesome or
some such thing.

Gary didn't care what Tim would call it. What he cared
about was that her slim-cut trousers made her legs seem
even longer than they were, and her blouse, visible because
he hadn't tied the jacket shut with those beaded strings,
ainted at the sweet curves of her breasts. Her hair was its
usual tousle of silver and gold curls, and her eyes sent him a
private message of warmth the instant he stepped into the
jury room.

En route to her side, he was waylaid by Jack Reilly, the
sandhog. "Hey, did you hear about Henri?" he asked.

"What about him?" Gary scanned the room in search of
Henri.

Before Jack could respond, one of the court officers appeared in the doorway. "Take your seats in the jury box," he announced. "The judge wishes to address you."

Had there been a settlement overnight? Gary thought hopefully. Or maybe a mistrial? Whatever it was, if it brought this nonsense to a close, Gary would be grateful. He'd gotten more than he'd ever dreamed of when he'd been summoned to participate in the American system of justice. Now all he wanted was to pursue that dream a bit more vigorously.

The jurors filed into the courtroom, Sophie just steps ahead of him. It took all his willpower not to tip his head slightly and catch a whiff of her delicately scented shampoo, or to reach out and press his fingers to the small of her back. He shoved his hands into the pockets of his jeans—his cleanest pair; he was dressing to the nines for Sophie, with his best Irish tweed jacket, only ten years old, and the tie that Tim said was his least dorky—and edged along the second row of seats to his own place, right next to Sophie.

He shouldn't have reacted so powerfully to the sight of her legs, one crossed over the other at the knee. Yesterday she'd been wearing that skirt with the peekaboo slit, but today all he could see was black twill, outlining the seductive length of her thighs. He flashed on a memory of being trapped with her in the elevator yesterday, the heat of her legs as he moved his hand between them....

He let out a long, slow breath and willed his body to relax. Just one more day, God and the lawyers willing, and they would be out of here, all finished with this ridiculous trial.

The litigants themselves entered the courtroom with their lawyers, the lawyers looking pompous and the litigants bewildered. Then the judge entered from her chambers, her lips pursed as if she'd been sucking lemons. She took her seat, ignoring Kramer, McGuire and their briefcase-toting warriors, and turned to speak to the jury.

"We received word early this morning," she announced, "that Henri Darranet's wife suffered a cardiac episode overnight. She is currently at Beth Israel Hospital and her prognosis is good. However, Mr. Darranet has requested removal from the jury so that he may attend to his wife's medical needs. I have granted this request.

"This means that the jury no longer has an alternate. All six of you are now full jurors, and you will be expected to see this trial through its conclusion and bring in a verdict. Are there any questions?"

Next to him, Sophie looked stricken. Granted, a juror's wife's heart attack wasn't exactly happy news, but it wasn't as if Henri had been a blood relative. He was only a fellow juror, a near stranger. Besides, the judge had said the prognosis was good. Why did Sophie appear to be on the verge of tears?

"I feel so terrible for him," she whispered. "He's such a nice man."

Gary recalled that she and Henri had sat together on the return ride from the wedding chapel yesterday. Perhaps they'd hit it off. Perhaps Gary wasn't the only juror she'd connected with.

Oh, for heaven's sake—if she'd connected with Henri the way she'd connected with Gary, she would be thrilled to hear his wife was having a cardiac episode. But Gary couldn't believe there was much connection between the two. Other than that forty-five minute drive in a bus yesterday, Sophie had been with Gary constantly. He'd been the one trapped in the elevator with her. He'd been the one kissing her, touching her, making them both crazy with unconsummated lust. When had she been out of his sight?

When he'd dropped her off at her house last night. Maybe the instant he'd driven away, she'd been on the phone to Henri, inviting him to cruise on over in that big-city bus he drove....

Gary swallowed a laugh at his wild imaginings. He wasn't the sort of guy who went loony over a woman, no matter how much he wanted her. The word *jealousy* was missing from his vocabulary. He was a firm believer in honesty, and if a woman wasn't honest with him, she wasn't worth his time.

That was how it had been with Meg. No piece of paper, no ceremony, no mumbo-jumbo could do as much for a relationship as total trust. He had trusted Meg completely, and he had lived up to her trust, and theirs had been a terrific relationship.

In any case, Gary had no reason to believe Sophie cared for Henri in any particular way. She was obviously just one of those empathetic types. Her eyes had filled with tears for Jocelyn Kramer, too. Chances were, she would weep for Ronald McGuire when he testified today. She was the kind of woman whose emotions lay close to the surface.

Gary couldn't wait to get beneath the surface with her, to find out how deep those emotions ran.

McGuire's hired gun, Harrison, was shuffling a stack of papers with the flair of a blackjack dealer from Atlantic City. The judge declared the court in session and asked the defense to present its case. Harrison glanced up with a cocky smile.

"Yes, Your Honor. I'd like to call Ronald McGuire to the stand."

McGuire stood, swore on the Bible and took his seat in the witness chair to the judge's left. He looked more dapper than Gary, but significantly less dapper than Harrison, who must have been charging astronomical fees if his suit was anything to judge by. Gary didn't know much about high fashion, a fact obvious to anyone who met him, but he knew the difference between a two-thousand-dollar suit and a ten-year-old tweed blazer. He was equally impressed by Harrison's tasseled shoes, which were polished to a mirror sheen. Gary imagined that if Harrison looked down at his feet, he would see his own face reflected, with the tassels coming out of his nostrils.

He ordered his thoughts back into line. Sophie was leaning forward in her chair, intent and intense, her pencil poised above a blank page in her notepad. Ronald McGuire sat stiffly in the witness box, his eyes straight ahead.

"Mr. McGuire," Harrison began, "you were at one time engaged to marry the plaintiff, is that right?"

"Yes." McGuire's voice wavered slightly, as if he thought he ought to say, "Yes, sir." Gary wondered whether the guy had a background in the army. No civilian could have posture that perfect.

"Did you love Ms. Kramer?"

"I thought I did. But the closer we got to the wedding date, the more I began to question my feelings about her."

"Were you aware that she was making plans for a huge wedding?"

"Yes."

"Expensive plans?"

"Yes. But I wasn't thinking about the wedding so much as the marriage. She was more concerned with what the bridesmaids should wear than whether we were a good couple."

"Did you discuss your misgivings with her?"

"I tried to, but she never listened to me. She was too busy planning the wedding day. *Her* day, she used to call it."

"Why weren't you blunt with her? Why didn't you state unequivocally that you wanted to break the engagement?"

"Well, I tried to. I'm naturally a polite guy, but I tried to explain things as clearly as I could. She told me prewedding jitters were normal and I should stop worrying. I think she just didn't want to hear what I was saying. That's why I had to take such a drastic step. I swear, if I'd shown up at the chapel on the wedding day, she would have overruled me again and dragged me down the aisle. I saw no other way to get through to her. I didn't mean to hurt her, and I know she wound up hurt. But it hurt *me* that she never listened to me when I tried to tell her I didn't want this marriage."

Harrison appeared pleased. "No further questions," he said, dusting a microscopic speck of dust from the sleeve of his spiffy jacket before he smiled at Laudrey. "Your witness."

Gary glanced at Sophie's pad. The page was covered with notes. He couldn't read them from his angle—not without being conspicuous about it—and he knew he wasn't supposed to be privy to her thoughts at this stage, anyway. But he was honestly astonished that she could have found so much to write about what struck him as plain, straightforward testimony. For all Kramer's whining and weeping, McGuire seemed to have this one in the bag.

Still, there was the cross-examination to get through. Gary turned his attention back to the witness stand as Kramer's lawyer approached McGuire. "Mr. McGuire," Laudrey said after sending a haughty look toward Harrison, "you are a marketing manager at a computer software firm. Is that correct?"

"Yes."

"You have three people reporting to you, not counting support staff. Right?"

"Yes."

"When you need to make yourself understood to your subordinates, do you have any trouble expressing your wishes?"

"No."

"And yet you couldn't make yourself understood to Ms. Kramer? This one woman? You couldn't state your position in a clear way?"

"I tried."

"Is Ms. Kramer stupid? Is she hearing-impaired? Why couldn't you make yourself understood to her?"

"I don't know. She just didn't want to listen."

"Isn't it possible that you failed to express yourself in a way she could understand?"

"Objection!" Harrison thundered toward the judge.

"I withdraw the question," Laudrey said, then gave McGuire a barracuda smile. "When did you first propose marriage to Ms. Kramer?"

"I—uh—it was sort of something we both agreed to. It wasn't like I got down on my knees or anything."

"You both agreed to get married. Both of you. Not just her. Correct?"

McGuire squirmed. "Well, yeah. But lots of engagements break up before the marriage. We were trying out the idea, that's all."

"And when did you decide to try out the idea, Mr. Mc-Guire? About a year before the wedding?"

"Yes."

"Why?"

"Why what?"

"Why did you decide to try out the idea of marriage?"

"Well...like I said earlier. I thought I loved her."

"You *thought* you loved her," Laudrey emphasized, letting the words linger in the still courtroom air for a minute before he continued. "Before that moment, you'd been dating Ms. Kramer for how long?"

"About a year, I guess. A little more than a year."

"So you'd been dating her for more than a year, contemplating the idea of marriage, and you weren't even sure you loved her?"

"Well...I thought I did."

"You couldn't make up your mind?" When McGuire squirmed again, glancing uncertainly past Laudrey at his own lawyer, Laudrey pressed him. "You, Mr. McGuire, a business executive with an M.B.A., a man used to making important decisions and taking actions, couldn't make up your mind about this?"

"I guess...love is hard, you know? It's hard to put your finger on it."

"And yet you agreed to marry her, anyway."

"Well, she wanted it, and I wanted to make her happy. She

really wanted to get married. We'd been dating long enough, she said. A whole year. I guess she sort of gave me an ultimatum— marry her or get lost."

"And you didn't want to break up with her then."

"I would have been happy to keep things as they were, you know? Just keep dating. Maintain the status quo."

"In other words, you liked sleeping with her without making any commitments."

"Objection!" Harrison roared.

Laudrey barreled ahead. "But you lacked the backbone to tell her that, Mr. McGuire, so when she pressed you for a commitment, you said yes. Is that correct?"

"I—well—I mean, I wouldn't put it that way."

"You wouldn't," Laudrey agreed. "But it's the truth."

Gary glanced at Sophie. Her pen was moving so rapidly along the lines of notepaper, her fingers blurred across his peripheral vision. He still couldn't decipher her handwriting from his angled view, but he had to admit that Laudrey had done some damage to McGuire. Not enough to destroy the guy's defense, but he'd succeeded in portraying McGuire as a stereotypical single guy, immature and irresponsible, an adherent of the old "Why buy the cow when you can get the milk for free?" philosophy of male-female relationships.

But being a typical single guy wasn't a crime. Lots of men endured marriage pressure from their girlfriends. McGuire was one of the rare ones, who at the last minute had refused to knuckle under. Did that mean he deserved to be sued?

This was why marriage was such a farce, Gary thought. People got married for a zillion different reasons, few of which had anything to do with love and commitment. Yet if the love was there, and the commitment, none of the rest mattered.

"No further questions," Laudrey declared, sharing a conspiratorial grin with the jury.

"Your next witness, Mr. Harrison?" the judge asked.

"No further witnesses," Harrison responded, sending his own confident smile in the jury's direction. "The defense rests."

Gary ruminated. Laudrey had done a decent job, but he hadn't persuaded Gary that McGuire owed his ex-fiancée anything more than a share of the wedding expenses and a gigantic apology. Sure, the guy was a knucklehead, sure, he was a bastard. But shouldn't Jocelyn Kramer be counting her blessings that he spared her a lifetime of marital misery?

Gary supposed he ought to wait until both attorneys had given their closing arguments before he made up his mind. Yet what was left to consider? A lady got jilted at the altar. Sad, yes. Humiliating, absolutely. But million-dollar tragic? No way. The only thing that made this trial worthy of Gary's time, he contemplated with a sidelong glance at the juror seated to his left, was the juror seated to his left.

She still had her legs crossed, one thigh slashing across the other in a sloping line that led his eyes upward into X-rated territory. He U-turned, tracing the leg with his gaze until he reached her foot, which jiggled with nervous energy. Her shoes were black suede, with pointed toes and random leather straps crisscrossing her insteps.

God. Her foot, shod in that odd suede contraption, was as erotic a sight as the place where his visual tour of her legs had begun.

He remembered her warmth last night, sexy but more than

sexy. She'd seemed so comfortable in his dining room, chatting with Tim and Pop, ambling through the orchard with his dogs. She'd tolerated Socrates and Plato, which was more than he could say for his own father. And her kisses... Her kisses were full of promise.

That promise would be realized as soon as this blasted trial was over. Just hours from now, perhaps. How long would two closing arguments take? Gary was positive the deliberations wouldn't last more than a half hour, even if they took a moment to pray for Henri's wife first. They could have this gig wrapped up in time for dinner. And after dinner...

After dinner, the world's greatest country mouse/city mouse romance could begin in earnest.

"LET US START BY TAKING a preliminary vote," Miss Prinz said once the jurors were shut inside the small jury room. "I shall hand out ballots. We shall start by determining whether we want to find for plaintiff or defendant before we begin to discuss the monetary ramifications of our verdict."

Sophie's ankle clenched. She hadn't been able to stop wiggling her foot since Ronald McGuire had immersed himself in his testimony. The creep! He was obviously a graduate of the Mitchell School of Immaturity, and with the help of her fine fellow jurors, she was going to see him suffer for it.

She had to believe Louise and Miss Prinz would find for Jocelyn Kramer. Miss Prinz had such a dour disposition, she must have been hurt by people—male people, no doubt—in her past. And Louise was so gentle and homey, surely she couldn't help but sympathize with a woman like Jocelyn, who wanted no more out of life than exactly what Louise had: a husband and a home.

The men were harder to read. Phillip the gym teacher seemed like a righteous sort, a bit brusque and reticent, but the kind of person who would know right from wrong. Jack the sandhog would vote with anyone who'd give him some free food. Indeed, he was already getting into an argument with Miss Prinz about how the jury should send out for sandwiches before they took any votes.

And then there was Gary. A devoted father, a devoted son. A man of the soil. A man of infinite patience. A man who had to possess rock-solid values. A man who believed in honesty above all. Surely he would recognize what a hypocrite Ronald McGuire was, and he would cast his vote for Jocelyn Kramer.

The balloting would be over in as little time as it took to unfold and tally six pieces of paper, and then they could leave. She and Gary could go somewhere....

Heat rushed up into her cheeks and down into her soul. He sat next to her, as he always did, his tall, lanky body folded into the chair beside hers and his legs extended in such a way that his knee was less than an inch from hers. All she had to do was hiccup, and their legs would be touching.

She'd better not get the hiccups. Her skin felt so feverish, she might just erupt in flames if her body came in contact with his.

"Mr. Reilly, I don't think sandwiches are as important as finding out where we stand at the start of deliberations," Miss Prinz chided.

"Yeah, but if we send out for sandwiches, the county pays," Jack argued.

"If you want a sandwich you'll have to earn it by casting a vote." With barely repressed hostility, Miss Prinz handed him a small square of paper, then softened slightly as she distributed papers to the rest of the jurors. "No consultations, please," she instructed them, as if they were about to tackle the College Boards and not a simple up-or-down vote on the verdict. "Do not talk to each other. Do not look at each other's votes."

"Use a number two pencil and fill in the blanks completely," Gary muttered under his breath. Sophie smothered a laugh. Just knowing that his thoughts mirrored hers gave her inordinate pleasure.

All six jurors bent over their ballots, marked them and folded them. Sophie slid hers to Gary, who added his ballot and hers to Phillip's. Miss Prinz collected them, then Louise's, Jack's and her own. Methodically, she unfolded each one and studied it.

Sophie eyed Gary, who was grinning at her. Was he still thinking what she was thinking—not about college admissions tests but about what was going to happen once the trial ended? Would he like to visit her shop, perhaps? Would he enjoy a taste of the city as much as she'd enjoyed a taste of the country? Would he want to come back to her apartment? Would she let him cross the bedroom threshold this time?

Would he kiss her the way he'd kissed her in the orchard, or on the elevator, or both? Would he touch her the way he'd touched her before, consoling and arousing, demanding yet giving her more than she could possibly ask for? Would he make love to her the way he did everything else—forcefully, playfully, groaning with passion and sighing with satisfaction?

"It seems we've got some work to do," Miss Prinz announced. "Right now, our balloting shows that five of us are leaning toward a finding for the plaintiff, and one of us supports the defendant."

"You're kidding!" Sophie blurted out. "Who could vote in favor of that dirt bag?"

Next to her, Gary drew himself up and flexed his shoulders. "Obviously, the only person on this jury who used his brain. I *do* have my work cut out for me, don't I?"

Sophie gaped at him in astonishment. Gary? Gary had voted for McGuire? "You're not going to convince *me* to change my vote," she retorted. "I wouldn't vote for that son of a gun if my life depended on it."

"That son of a gun spared Ms. Waterworks Kramer from a horrible marriage. He deserves a medal, not a judgment against him."

"He broke an agreement—to say nothing of breaking her heart!"

"So, big deal. Let him kick in toward the unpaid bills. Beyond that, what does she want from him—a pound of flesh? This case is a bad joke, and voting for the woman who inflicted it on us would be an even worse joke."

"*You're* a joke," Sophie raged. "I can't believe you'd take his side! I thought you were a good man."

"And I thought you were a smart woman!"

"Can we order out for sandwiches now?" Jack asked hopefully.

Sophie shifted her chair away from Gary. Her foot vibrated in double time, and the way she was feeling toward him, it wouldn't take much conscious effort on her part to slam that moving foot right into his stupid, macho, hick-farmer shin. So what if he loved his kid and took care of his dad? So what if he had two endearingly dopey dogs? Of the three men in the jury room, only one had sympathized with the kind of bastard who would jilt his sweetheart on her wedding day.

It was Sophie's wretched luck that the juror who would take Ronald McGuire's side in the battle would be the man she'd fallen in love with.

8

FOUR HOURS LATER, the six jurors in the cramped little room had devoured a platter of deli sandwiches, a bowl of fruit, a box of chocolate-chip cookies, several gallons of coffee and a six-pack of diet cola. And Louise had changed her mind.

"I don't know, the more I think about it, the more I figure a bad marriage is worse than no marriage at all," she said, her tone defensively whiny. "Maybe Jocelyn Kramer should be thanking Mr. McGuire instead of suing him."

"Good point," Jack Reilly agreed cheerfully. He was in no hurry to reach a verdict. As long as he was a juror, he could sit around on his duff and continue to collect his hefty union wage. "Seems to me, though, that if we're going to keep arguing about this, we ought to check out whether the court could send in some brewskies. I always have a cold one around this hour of the day. I'd hate to go through withdrawal."

"The jury process requires sobriety," Miss Prinz reminded him, pursing her lips in distaste.

"I wasn't planning to get drunk. All I want is just one dose. Whaddya say, Phillip? You want to join me in a bit of libation?"

"I want to jog," Phillip growled.

"Gary?" Jack persisted. "You up for a beer?"

Gary shrugged. "I'm up for bringing about justice, that's all."

Hypocrite, Sophie thought furiously. *Two-faced jerk!* How could he cast his lot with a man who snubbed his bride on her wedding day? How could he side with a man like Ronald McGuire?

How could Sophie ever have thought she loved him?

"There will be no beer," Miss Prinz declared firmly. "Not until after we've delivered a verdict."

"Which could be next year, the way things are going," Phillip grumbled.

The jury had rearranged itself around the table so many times, they might have been mistaken for square dancers. Right now, Sophie was seated next to Phillip near what would be the foot of the table, assuming Miss Prinz was seated at the head. After his last refill of coffee, Gary had wound up directly across from Sophie. His jaw was darkened by a stubble of beard, his tie hung loose and his collar button was undone. He'd removed that godawful tweed jacket some time ago and rolled up the sleeves of his shirt. He looked like the night editor at a tabloid newspaper, holding the presses until he could run a tawdry scandal on the front page. The banner headline could read Man Jilts Bride-To-Be, Wins Respect Of Juror.

Really, how could Sophie have fallen for him? How could she have been snookered by his wholesome household—his sweet, clumsy dogs, his dad and his adorable son? How could she have believed he was better than the average male?

Gary Brett was a cad. A cur. A despicable brute.

Too bad he looked so unforgivably gorgeous.

She couldn't help but suspect that Louise had changed her mind for no other reason than Gary's smile. Sophie knew the potency of that smile; it was a smile that had beguiled her into thinking she was in love with him. He'd been wielding his smile ever since they'd retired to the jury room after closing arguments. Seated right across from Louise for much of the discussion, he'd probably been bombarding her with invisible support-the-defendent dimple rays.

"Here's what I think," Phillip growled, growling apparently being his favorite mode of communication. "I think we should tell the judge we're hopelessly deadlocked."

"We will not be a hung jury," Miss Prinz declared.

"Some of us jurors already are hung," Jack quipped, shooting a wicked grin Gary's way.

A smile flickered across Gary's face but didn't linger. Evidently he considered this verdict a serious matter.

As did Sophie. She wasn't ready to concede defeat—either to the pro-McGuire forces or to the clock. It was just barely eight o'clock. Surely Gary—and now Louise—could be brought to their senses if Sophie, Phillip and Miss Prinz worked on them a little bit longer.

"I really don't think you guys are considering what Jocelyn Kramer has been through," Sophie said. "McGuire deliberately found the most hurtful way to break up with her. Even under the best circumstances, getting dumped by a lover is devastating. And the way McGuire did it—"

"That's about the tenth time you've said that," Gary complained.

"You obviously weren't listening the first nine times," she said, her tone dripping with venom.

His gaze narrowed on her. "You know, a person could be

forgiven for thinking maybe you were speaking from experience. Getting dumped by a lover in the most hurtful way... I don't know, Sophie. Are you attaching some personal significance to all this?"

None of your business, she wanted to reply. If Gary wanted to know about her experiences, it could only be because he was planning to use the information to undermine her, either here in the jury room or elsewhere: in an orchard or a broken elevator, perhaps. Whatever his agenda was—to seduce her, to demolish her, to punish her for having fought him over the jury foreman thing—she couldn't begin to guess. All she knew was that she no longer trusted the man who claimed honesty was everything in a relationship.

On the other hand, Miss Prinz had no hidden agenda. "If you could offer a fresh perspective, Sophie," she admonished, "it might help to move things along."

Sophie sighed. "Well, I said it during voir dire. I've been dumped by a man. You all know that."

"And you survived," Gary pointed out. "You flourished. You look magnificent, you've got a happy life, a terrific career—"

"None of us is going to have a career if we don't wrap this thing up soon," Phillip muttered.

"I am," Jack interjected. "They can't fire me for serving on a jury. It's the law. I'm in the union."

"My career is irrelevant to this trial," Sophie asserted, as impatient as Phillip. She just wanted to get the deliberations over with, so she could go home and see if Lynn's buddy, the investment banker with the vacation house on the Vineyard, was still available. "If you want the dirt on my private life, if you really think that would make a difference—"

"Inquiring minds want to know," Jack quipped, sparing Gary the necessity of having to admit his own curiosity.

Still, if it would accelerate the process so she could get the hell out of here, away from Gary and his disturbing smile, and his bedroom eyes, and her memories of his hands on her, his lips on her...

"I moved to Cambridge from California because the man I loved was originally from Boston and he asked me to marry him. He'd been summoned back home to take his place in his father's firm. So I sold my business in San Francisco and closed up my apartment and followed him here. And then his hoity-toity family decided I wasn't good enough for him, and he broke the engagement."

"Oh, that's terrible!" Louise's voice crackled with indignation. "What a terrible thing to do! After you'd burned all your bridges! You poor dear!"

"Trust me, it *was* terrible," Sophie said, ignoring Louise's gushing pity in an effort to drive her point home with all the jurors. "It was agony. And Jocelyn—"

"But," Louise continued, "you've got to admit this terrible man spared you from a bad marriage."

"I'm not so sure it would have been a bad marriage," Sophie insisted, refusing to back down when there was the slimmest chance she might convert Louise. "Mitchell and I loved each other. Everyone who knew us in California thought we made the perfect couple—and I thought we did, too. And I assume he thought so, too. He wouldn't have asked me to marry him if he didn't."

"But if this marriage wasn't meant to be—"

"We had talked about marriage for months before we agreed to go ahead with it. It wasn't something we'd decided on as a whim. We discussed the kind of wedding we wanted. He had a strong attachment to his parents' church, so we decided to tie the knot in Boston. It was going to be a very traditional wedding. A sacred ceremony, drenched in tradition."

"Sounds to me like you dodged a bullet," Gary remarked wryly.

"Well, what would you know?" she retorted. "You've dumped women left and right."

He frowned in indignation. "I never said that."

"You implied as much during voir dire."

"All I said is, these things are never one-sided. Your fiancé—Mitchell, was that his name? He may have broken up with you, but I'm sure you contributed to the breakup."

"How did I contribute? I sacrificed my home, my store, my friends—everything for him."

"And maybe he discovered he didn't want a pushover. He wanted someone who *wouldn't* give up everything for him."

"I'm not a pushover!"

"I don't think Sophie's a pushover," Louise asserted, turning to Jack. "Do you?"

"I don't know. She seems kind of like a spitfire to me."

"She's not a spitfire," Phillip argued. "She's more of a dynamo."

"A dynamo?" Miss Prinz regarded Sophie critically. "I don't know. I think *militant* would be the word that best describes her. All that note-taking and belligerence."

"Since when are militancy and dynamism mutually exclusive?" Phillip asked.

"Oh, for heaven's sake!" Unable to sit still while she was dissected by five court-selected idiots, Sophie pushed herself to her feet and pounded the table with her fist. "This isn't about me. It's about Jocelyn Kramer and Ronald McGuire. If you people don't get back on track, I'm going to ask the judge to declare a mistrial."

"We will not have a mistrial," Miss Prinz decreed. "Even if some jurors seem to think they're...hung." Her pasty cheeks flushed with unexpected color as she alluded to Jack's earlier joke.

"If we're not having a mistrial, then let's have a beer," Jack suggested.

"If we're going to be here much longer," Gary said quietly, his eyes never leaving Sophie as she resumed her seat, "I'd like to call home and let my family know I'm going to be late."

"Why call them?" Sophie countered. "Why not solve this damned thing now, and we can all leave." *In separate elevators*, she added silently.

"Let's give it until nine o'clock," Miss Prinz said. "If we haven't reached a verdict by then, we'll confer with the judge."

BY 9:00 P.M., they were nowhere near reaching a verdict. Jack complained of suffering from brewskie-withdrawal. Phillip was power-walking in circles around the small room. The three women huddled at the blackboard, chalking numbers and calendar dates as if the fact that the Kramers had lost money on the aborted wedding justified Jocelyn's jacked-up claims of pain and suffering.

Sure, losing money was a drag. But if losing money was legally actionable, lottery losers would be suing the state every day.

None of which seemed anywhere near as significant to Gary as Sophie's revelations about her own romantic past. So, she'd been in the market for a big, splashy wedding. A sacred, traditional one, at Mitchell's snooty family church in Boston. If everything had gone as planned, Sophie would have had herself one hell of an extravaganza.

Obviously, she and Gary had very different values.

So why did his blood still run hot through his veins when he looked at her? Why did merely thinking about her make his jeans feel snug? Why, when he tried to convince himself that she was all wrong for him, did his memory keep veering back to yesterday, to the way she'd gotten along with Tim and Pop and the dogs, the way she'd glowed with contentment as he'd strolled with her through the orchard...the way she'd kissed him, and melted against him, and sighed and gasped and burned for him in the elevator? Why did all that make her seem so right?

Well, one thing she wasn't right about was this trial. If Jocelyn Kramer was going to wrench him out of his daily life with her ridiculous lawsuit, and waste the court's time and the taxpayers' money, then he was going to show the plaintiff the error of her ways. All he needed to do was bring the rest of this jury around to his way of thinking.

"Let's back up a minute," Miss Prinz was saying. "I thought Mr. McGuire had paid for the flowers."

"Wrong." Sophie flipped through her notepad, searching for the entry. "Ah, here it is. Flowers—seven hundred thirty-five dollars, billed to the Kramers."

"Seven hundred thirty-five buckaroos for flowers?" Jack whispered to Gary. "Can you believe it?"

"And then, three days later, all those flowers would be dead," Gary whispered back.

"I don't think we spent that much on flowers for my uncle's funeral. No more than maybe a hundred, a hundred-fifty tops."

"It's crazy. Who needs so many flowers? What do flowers have to do with 'til death do us part?"

"I still think Sophie's a spitfire, though," Jack observed, sotto voce. "What do you think? You think a lady like that would get turned on by flowers?"

"Who the hell knows what would turn her on?" Gary snapped irritably, even though he had a few specific ideas about what turned her on.

A rap on the door connecting the jury room to the courtroom interrupted his thoughts about how very much he'd like to turn Sophie on, with or without flowers. The door opened and a uniformed officer peered in. "It's nearly ten o'clock. How are we doing in here?" he asked.

Miss Prinz turned from the blackboard. "We're deliberating," she said.

"We're hung," Jack called to the officer, then nudged Gary in the ribs.

The officer asked Miss Prinz, "Are you anywhere near a verdict?"

"No," six voices chorused in reply.

"The judge is in no mood to declare a mistrial. She feels you should be able to reach a verdict in this case."

"Well, we can't," Sophie wailed. "Can't we just call it a mistrial and go home?"

"You can go home," the officer said, "but you'll have to return at 8:00 a.m. and resume deliberations."

"Why 8:00 a.m.?" Gary protested. "Who says we've got to get here so early?"

"The judge," the officer said simply. "Come on into the courtroom so you can be officially dismissed for the night."

"I don't want to come back here tomorrow," Sophie grumbled under her breath. Gary heard her, though. His antennae were tuned to the Sophie channel. He could practically hear her thoughts—and they were that it wasn't the jury room she didn't want to come back to. It was Gary.

Well, there was a simple enough way for her to avoid coming back: change her vote. He knew how persuasive she could be, and he was positive that if she switched sides, Jack would fall into line. It sounded as if he was half in love with her already.

Spitfire, Gary thought grimly. He couldn't sway Jack, but the spitfire could. Of course, if Gary bribed Jack with a can of beer...

Jack was flexible. Phillip just wanted to jog and bark at his students in Billerica. Miss Prinz... Gary couldn't begin to guess where she stood anymore. The only time she participated in the discussion was to announce a point of order or to scold someone for misbehaving.

All right. It looked as if they were in for another spell at the county courthouse tomorrow. Gary could tolerate it. Sophie would just have to.

HER TOLERANCE LEVEL was dangerously low as they left the courtroom and headed for the elevator bank. She stood as far from Gary as she could, but as usual only one elevator seemed to be working, and all six jurors boarded together. Gary let her take the left rear corner and discreetly shifted toward the right so she wouldn't accidentally have to brush against him. Louise spent the entire descent babbling about how the last time she'd stayed out this late was when her husband's boss invited the entire sales staff to a restaurant in Waltham, and she and her husband would have gotten home earlier but their car battery died. "This is more exciting," she blathered.

More exciting than a dead battery? Gary didn't think so. He was too irked by Sophie's moodiness. Just because he happened to disagree with her on this trial was no reason for her to view him as her enemy. They could disagree without losing what they had, couldn't they?

He didn't think Sophie was afraid of a fight. Fighting with her over the jury foreman's job hadn't brought on any lasting animosity. If anything, that squabble had cranked up the heat between them a few degrees—which had suited him just fine.

No, he knew what was eating her: not that Gary disagreed with her, but that Gary would side with a guy who had done to a woman what some other nitwit had done to Sophie. When it came to Jocelyn Kramer, Sophie wasn't thinking. She was feeling, reliving her own lousy experience with Boston-Brahman Mitchell. She was empathizing with Jocelyn instead of using logic to see the situation for what it was. Hadn't McGuire's lawyer opened with the old saw about hell having no fury like a woman scorned? Sophie had been scorned once, and now she was going to make McGuire pay.

And Gary, too, apparently.

This was why he had no use for marriage. It seemed obvious to him that whatever grief Sophie had suffered at Mitchell's hands had less to do with the guy than with the wedding that never was. If they'd loved each other, whether or not his parents had approved, whether Sophie and Mitchell had settled on the East Coast or the West, whether they'd exchanged vows in this church or that—none of it would have mattered.

Mix a wedding into the equation, and all it did was screw everything up.

The elevator's doors slid open at the ground floor. Gary lingered several paces behind Sophie as she stalked across the lobby and through the metal detector, arranged her colorful woven jacket on her shoulders and shoved open the door to the street. Outside on the sidewalk, she hesitated.

It was late, and the street was empty. Nary a cab was in sight.

"I'll give you a lift," he said, sidling up behind her.

"Don't do me any favors."

"Come on, Sophie. You aren't going to get a cab at this hour. And forget public transit."

"It's only a little after ten."

"It's dark. I'll drive you home."

He could practically hear the crunch of her gnashing teeth. No matter how much she resented him—no matter how much she resented the entire male half of the species—she had enough sense not to go traipsing around the desolate downtown neighborhood after hours, hoping a cab might miraculously appear. "All right," she said curtly. She couldn't even spare him a thank-you.

Gary didn't mind. He wasn't giving her a lift because he wanted her thanks. What he wanted from her had nothing to do with gratitude.

They walked down the block to the garage together, not

talking, not touching. A car horn echoed in the distance, a melancholy drone that emphasized his isolation from Sophie, and hers from him. As they passed beneath a mercury lamp, her hair looked almost pink in the eerie light, a maze of tangled tendrils beckoning his fingers.

He shoved his hands into his pockets.

He and Sophie reached the garage, climbed the steps to the third level and located his car. In silence, he unlocked the passenger door and opened it, then succumbed to the chivalrous urge to touch her arm as she lowered herself into the bucket seat. He felt the woolly texture of her jacket and the sharp angle of her elbow—but more than that, he felt a jolt of arousal. It was like tripping a latch and letting a long-suppressed beast spring from its cage.

Damn it, he wanted her. Even if she was royally ticked. Even if her rantings about McGuire and wedding flowers and her own thwarted marriage were irrational. Even if she hated Gary's guts.

He wanted her.

A self-protective impulse compelled him to close her door and take a deep breath before circling the car to climb into the driver's seat. Once he was behind the wheel, she would be barely inches from him, her soft perfume filling his nostrils, her body and breath altering the atmosphere. But he was a big boy. He'd suffered worse disappointments in his life than blowing his chances with an artsy Cambridge shop owner. Whatever discomfort he'd feel driving her to her apartment was trivial compared to the discomfort he would have felt if he'd left her to fend for herself on that barren city block.

He steered out of the garage and headed west through the

city. Sophie sat rigidly in her seat, her hands folded in her lap and waves of tension radiating from her like UVs from the sun, invisible but carcinogenic. When he stopped at a red light and shifted into neutral, he could have sworn he heard her sob, but when he glanced her way, she appeared stony-eyed.

The light turned green and he pressed the gas pedal. He heard the sound again—a damp sort of sigh.

Panic seized him, tightening like a knot in his throat. He did not want to deal with a weepy woman in his car. He had no patience for that sort of nonsense. One of the things that had turned him off to Jocelyn Kramer's situation was her gallons-of-tears routine on the stand.

At least Sophie wasn't bawling. She pressed her lips together so they couldn't tremble, and her eyes glistened but didn't overflow. Even in her lap, her hands didn't flutter. She was so composed, he began to think maybe the noise he'd mistaken for a sob was actually air seeping from one of his tires.

He became acutely conscious of the car's sounds: the motor's hum, the whisper of the ventilation system, the click of the directional signal...and that sigh again, plaintive and heart-wrenching.

"Okay," he muttered, pulling into the first parking space he saw on her street. "What?"

"What?" she answered dryly.

"You're sighing."

"Excuse me?"

"You're sighing."

"I am *not* sighing."

"I heard you."

"Good night, Gary." She reached for the door lever.

He grabbed her hand to stop her from leaving—and then, once his hand closed around hers, he knew he wasn't going to let go. "What? What terrible thing did I do, that you're treating me like I'm toxic?"

"You didn't *do* anything," she answered, her tone measured, her words crisp. "You're a man, Gary. You can't help it if your Y chromosomes have screwed up your thinking."

"My Y chromosomes are my best feature," he argued.

"Then you have my sympathy. Good night."

"Sophie. Please." He couldn't believe he was begging her to stay in the car with him a minute longer. But his hand seemed locked into position around hers, unable to relent and let her leave. Her skin was too smooth, too soft. Her eyes were too beautiful, too luminous. Her resentment of him was too palpable. "What about yesterday?" he attempted. "I thought you had a good time with me out in Stow."

"That was before…" She caught herself and clamped her mouth shut.

"Before what?"

"I'm not going to discuss the trial with you, Gary. We're not allowed to talk about it outside of court."

"Forget about the trial. This is about us."

"What's about us?"

"It's about you've got a chip on your shoulder the size of Idaho because some jerk dumped you. *I* didn't dump you, Sophie. *I'm* not the guy who called off your nuptials."

"You're in league with a guy who called off his nuptials. Damn," she muttered, clapping her free hand to her mouth. "We're really not supposed to talk about the trial, Gary."

"I don't give a rat's behind about the trial. For that matter,

I don't give a rat's behind about the guy in Boston. Mitchell, was it? He's history, okay?"

Slowly she lowered her hand from her lips. Rosy and sweet, they mesmerized Gary with their movements as she spoke. "He's *my* history. My lesson in life. If you think what he did was acceptable, then you're no better than he is."

"I didn't say what he did was acceptable."

"You implied it. What he did to me wasn't all that different from what...*somebody* did to *somebody*," she said carefully, avoiding mention of McGuire and Kramer. "And since you seem to think that what *somebody* did to *somebody* is no big deal—"

"I'm not saying he's right. I'm just saying she hasn't got a case."

"Don't talk about it."

Fine. He didn't want to sit in his car with her, bickering about history lessons, or alluding obliquely to the trial and then feeling guilty and backtracking because that subject was off-limits. If he was going to talk to Sophie, he wanted to talk to her about her store, or his son's baseball team, or how progressive rock music stank compared to the music of the Eagles. He wanted to talk to her about how her skin felt like the petals of an apple blossom—pale and smooth and delicate.

Actually, he didn't really want to talk. He wanted to kiss her. Whether she despised all people with Y chromosomes didn't matter. Whether she was still nursing grudges from some old love-and-war injury was irrelevant. Whether she and Gary would face off tomorrow morning in the jury room, no closer to finding common ground for a verdict in Kramer v. McGuire, had no bearing on what was going to happen tonight.

He leaned across the gear stick, slid his hand under the lush mane of curls at the nape of her neck and lowered his mouth to hers.

9

IF SHE HADN'T ALREADY hated him, she would hate him for this: his ability to erase all her hatred with one single, searing kiss. As his lips covered hers, brushed and grazed and nipped at hers, her anger seemed to evaporate into a faint mist that rose from her soul and vanished into the air.

Had she resented him? Why? Something about the trial, maybe...the trial she wasn't supposed to think about.

Well, she wouldn't think about it, then. As long as Gary was kissing her, she would think only about what a good man he was, a loving father, a dependable son, a man solid to the core, noble and decent, a man of honor. She would think about how strong he was, how sensitive, how stalwart...how stunningly sensual.

She sank against the soft leather of the bucket seat as Gary leaned closer. He dug his fingers into her hair, holding her head still as his mouth moved over hers, again and again, sweet and slow. She felt his warmth, felt the absence of him where the space limitations of the car prevented him from pulling her into his arms or settling his body over hers. The layer of air between her chest and his nearly drove her crazy.

Since she couldn't haul him over the console and into her lap, she did what she could. She circled her hands around his shoulders and opened her mouth to him, and sighed with pleasure as his tongue met hers.

What on earth could she have been so angry about? This was Gary. The finest, kindest, sexiest man she'd ever met. A man of convictions, true—but she admired that. A man who held fast to his values. A man who spoke his mind and obeyed his heart.

He eased out of the kiss and let out a ragged breath. "Sophie," he murmured, her name floating from his lips to hers.

"Yes." She might have meant her answer as a simple acknowledgment that she'd heard him, or as an invitation for him to continue what he wanted to say. But he seemed to interpret her *yes* another way, and she realized she might just have intended it that other way. Yes, she wanted his kisses. Yes, she wanted him.

Yes.

Somehow, he broke from her long enough to get out of the car. Mere seconds later, he was yanking open the passenger door and helping her to her feet. A twist of his key locked the vehicle, and then they raced toward her building, her hand in his, her heart pounding as if she'd just jogged up Heartbreak Hill on the Boston Marathon route.

Yes, she thought. The disagreements of the jury room didn't matter—not now. All that mattered was Gary, the need she'd seen in his eyes, the matching need that swelled inside her, whispering: "Yes."

Inside the door of her apartment, she paused to catch her breath—and he paused to kiss her again. This kiss was deeper, fuller. Unconstrained by seat belts and gear sticks, they could wrap their arms around each other, press their bodies together and let the heat burn brighter. Gary's lips urged hers apart and his tongue slid deep, filling her, withdrawing and filling her again. Her knees trembled and she closed her eyes, almost embarrassed by the flood of desire throbbing through her.

Why had she resisted this? What on earth had she been so upset about?

She couldn't remember. She could scarcely think at all— except about this, about Gary, about how much she needed him.

After thoroughly conquering her mouth, Gary moved upward, kissing the tip of her nose, the bridge, her brow. "I should call home," he murmured, his hands roaming restlessly through her hair. "I don't want them to worry."

How could she have thought he was anything but the most decent, honest, trustworthy family man in the universe? "I've got a phone in the bedroom," she said, startling herself. She had a phone in the kitchen, too. He'd used it just yesterday, when he'd called to warn his family that he was bringing her to his house for dinner. But her kitchen was not the room preoccupying her right now. Her mind was firmly fixed on the bedroom.

He rested his forehead against hers, his arms wrapped loosely around her shoulders and his lips curved in a smile. She smiled, too. As excited as she was, as wildly as she wanted him, she was also content. Happy, even. Passion and joy made good partners, and everything about this moment and this man felt so right, she couldn't help grinning.

Releasing her, he let her lead him down the hall. She preceded him into her bedroom, clicked on a bedside lamp and gestured toward the phone on the nightstand. He followed her in almost shyly, respectful of what it meant for her to allow him in. If she was going to suffer misgivings, it ought to happen now, as he breached the threshold, as he crossed the room to her side.

No misgivings. Only more joy, more certainty that this was the right thing to do, and Gary Brett was the right man.

He looped his arm around her shoulder as he reached for the phone. The way he held her close, as if she belonged by his side, in the curve of his arm, let her know that he wanted her with him while he made his call. A glance at her alarm clock told her it was not yet 10:30 p.m.

"Hello? It's me, Pop.... I'm still in Cambridge. The judge just dismissed us a few minutes ago, but we've got to report back tomorrow at eight. I was figuring, under the circumstances, that I'd spend the night in town." He glanced at Sophie, then touched his lips to the crown of her head. Evidently his father said something, because he turned back to the phone. "No, no verdict yet.... I know Tim's got a game Saturday. If this trial isn't over by then, I'll feign a stroke and force them to excuse me. Okay?... Yeah, tell Tim I love him. No, don't give him a hug for me. It'll only embarrass him. Just tell him I said to make sure he does all his homework. And don't forget to feed the dogs tomorrow morning. I mean it, Pop. If they starve to death in my absence, I'm reporting you to the animal welfare people." He laughed, then said good-night and lowered the phone.

Easing Sophie around in his arms, he kissed her again, a light, teasing kiss. "I'm trying to think of everything before I lose my mind," he said.

"What are you trying to think of?"

He kissed her again, then peered into her eyes. "Protection?" he half asked. "I wasn't planning on this, Sophie. I didn't exactly come prepared."

Her love for him seemed to grow exponentially. He was so solicitous of his father, his son and his dogs, so concerned for her safety.... She was close to losing her mind, too. "I'm sure I have a box somewhere," she told him. "If I can only remember where I put it."

He chuckled. "How could you not remember?"

"Well, I don't—I haven't..." Flustered, she turned from him and yanked open the nightstand drawer, hoping in vain that the package of condoms she'd bought ages ago would be there. She knew it wouldn't be, though. She poked around in that drawer often enough to know what was in it: her personal schedule book, notepads, a phone directory, a sewing kit and a variety of pens and pencils. Not what she and Gary needed.

"Maybe the bathroom," she said, straightening up.

His expression took her aback. He was studying her, only a shadow of his smile remaining, his eyes intense as he cupped his hand to her cheek. "You haven't used them recently, have you?"

"No," she admitted, because his gaze demanded honesty.

"I don't take this sort of thing lightly, either," he confessed.

The intimacy of the conversation disconcerted her. How odd that she could be raring to make love to him, yet to discuss their views of sex, their habits and yearnings seemed far more personal than tearing off their clothes and going at it.

She wasn't sure what to say. That she had assumed he *did* take it lightly? She hadn't really thought about it—except that he was a man, and men were supposed to be more casual about sex.

Had it been as long for him as for her? Had the last woman

he'd been with been as important to him as Mitchell had been to her? Was this whole thing doomed because neither of them was in practice?

"I guess we'll just fumble our way through it," she said, wishing she could get back to the giddy frenzy of a few minutes ago.

His smile returned, only it wasn't the same smile. This was a sheer male smile, dark and predatory and arrogant, a smile that sent shock waves of heat all the way down to her toes and up to her scalp. "No, Sophie," he promised. "We won't fumble at all."

She swallowed. In a tiny voice, she said, "I'll see if I can find that box."

She fled from the bedroom, hoping to collect her wits before she had to face him again. She'd never thought of herself as a femme fatale, a suave seductress luring men to her boudoir. But honestly, she didn't have to act like a blushing virgin, did she? Her brain must have suffered a complete meltdown.

She searched the medicine cabinet above the sink in the bathroom, and then the storage area under the sink. She found painkillers, half-used tubes of long-forgotten lipstick, enough bandages to supply a Civil War battlefield, cleansers, bottles of bubble bath she never had time to use…but no condoms. The linen closet in the hall had, besides the usual assortment of towels and sheets, a hair dryer, boxes of tissues, bags of toilet paper and four bottles of perfume, still in their original packaging, which her aunt Martha had sent her for Christmas the past four years. No condoms.

Taking a long, steady breath to compose herself, she reentered her bedroom. Gary was standing near the window, draping his tie over his blazer, which was spread over the arm of a chair. When he turned to her, she saw that his shirt was unbuttoned.

His chest. Her entire consciousness narrowed to the sleek strip of skin exposed where the shirt gaped open. That was Gary's skin. His torso. His body.

Her knees wobbled beneath the sudden, heavy warmth that settled in her hips. Oh—she was going to fumble, all right. She couldn't even glimpse an inch of his chest without losing her balance.

His face brightened with a smile. He glanced at her empty hands, then lifted his gaze back to hers. "No luck? I could run out to an all-night drugstore. Or—" his smile grew dangerous "—I could be creative."

She nearly staggered. "I still have one place to check," she mumbled, hurrying to her dresser. She yanked open the drawer that held her underwear. There, hidden amid the pastel-colored panties, she found the box.

"That looks interesting," Gary said, approaching the open drawer. He wasn't looking at the box, though. Her rose-hued camisole had caught his eye. Delicately he lifted the slip of silk from the drawer. "You wear this?"

"Sometimes." Her cheeks had to be the same color as the camisole. Something about the way he held the dainty garment in his large, work-hardened hands sent a shiver through her.

He lowered it back into the drawer, then discovered a pair of lacy cream-colored bikini panties. "These are nice, too."

"I don't think they'd fit you," she said.

He laughed. The sound relaxed her—until he dropped the panties and tugged his shirttail free of his jeans. Then she didn't feel terribly relaxed anymore. She felt keyed-up, tight and tingly, eager and panic-stricken and almost faint with longing. He gave voice to her thoughts as if they were his, as if her mind and his had become one. "I want you," he murmured, easing the box from her nervous fingers and tossing it onto the bed. Then he drew her hands inside the open flaps of his shirt and pressed them to his skin.

The feel of him was oddly nourishing, giving her strength and slaking her edginess. He felt so good, he looked so sincere...and he wanted her. So what if she fumbled? From the way he gazed at her, the way he felt beneath her fingertips, she knew her fumbling couldn't make him want her any less.

"I want you, too," she whispered. She ran her hands over the smooth skin of his chest. It felt like silk—not the silk of her lingerie, but thick, raw silk, warm and supple, stretching over sheets of sleek muscle that flexed and tightened against her palms. When she moved her hands down to the waist of his jeans, he groaned, low and dark in his throat.

He slid her jacket from her shoulders, then plucked open the buttons of her blouse with amazing efficiency. At the bottom edge of her blouse he kept going, working open the button and fly of her slacks. He nudged them down over her hips, out of his way, and then wedged his hands inside her panties. As fascinated as he'd been by the lingerie in her drawer, he didn't even bother to glance at what she had on. All he seemed to care about was stripping her naked.

His fingers skimmed down her belly and into the nest of hair between her legs. She whimpered, and he covered her mouth with his, kissing her deeply, entering her with his tongue as his fingers entered her below. She moaned, shocked by his aggressiveness and her own response, the

dense, lush pressure of needing him making her mind spin
and her heart sprint. "Gary..." She thought she was crying
out, but she couldn't hear herself. "Gary..." It was her heart
singing, her soul calling to him.

The next few seconds were a blur of snaps and zippers
coming undone, her bra falling away, his jeans, her socks, his
shirt. And then they were on the bed, Gary sprawled beside
her, tall and tough and gloriously naked. He smelled of soap
and sex. He tasted like mint and musk. His kisses devoured
her, his hands explored her and his body moved—a lithe,
masculine expanse for her to touch and savor.

Her caresses seemed to delight him. Her gentle—and then
not-so-gentle—kisses thrilled him, and thrilled her even
more. She nipped lightly at his shoulders, grazed to his chest
and flicked her tongue over his nipple.

He gasped and pressed her onto her back, then enacted his
own version of the golden rule, doing to her as she'd done to
him. He kissed her throat, her shoulders, her collarbones, her
breasts, suckling one and then the other until she could no
longer lie still. Her hips twisted against the blanket, her legs
shifted restlessly, and he found her with his hand again, then
teased and stroked and aroused her without mercy.

She writhed against him, clinging, kissing, aching as his
fingers lured her. Once again she was sure she was screaming his name. Once again she couldn't hear herself. But how
could she vocalize her pleasure when she seemed to have
forgotten how to breathe? Her voice lodged in her throat, her
lungs stopped functioning and every last spark of energy inside her surged downward, to his hand, to her soul.

It was too soon, they'd barely begun, she hadn't even
opened the damned box of condoms...and she was already

cresting, pulsing hot and fierce against his fingers. Mortified, she hid her face against his shoulder. She could feel the color flooding her cheeks. Talk about fumbling! She was a disaster!

"Sophie?" His voice reached her, hushed yet vibrating with suppressed laughter.

Great. He was laughing at her. He was thinking she was the most inept, impatient woman he'd ever made love to. He was thinking she was selfish and out of control, and...

"That was the appetizer," he murmured. "Think you can handle the main course?"

She dared to peek past her humiliation—and past his shoulder. With easy grace, he pulled back and reached for the box. In a moment he was looming above her, stretched long and taut, his face a mixture of amusement and adoration and unabashed lust. Not ridicule. Not dissatisfaction. Just Gary, wholehearted, one-hundred-percent Gary.

"Dare I ask what the main course is?" she questioned, groping for her sense of humor to get her through her embarrassment.

"Meat," he told her, pressing her legs apart with his knees plunging into her.

This time she heard her cry of surrender, of ecstasy, of astonishment that she could have lived thirty years of her life without ever having experienced something as right as this—Gary Brett, his love, his body locked within hers. How had she done it? How had she existed when such perfection had eluded her until this very moment?

They fit together, moved together, scaled the heights together. They breathed together, moaned together, linked their fingers together and arched and ground their hips together and sighed together. She leaned up to kiss him the exact instant he bowed to kiss her. She opened her eyes to see him opening his eyes. The moment she needed him faster he thrust faster; the moment she needed him harder and deeper, he pushed harder and deeper. She didn't have to tell him. He knew.

The main course, indeed. This was gourmet heaven.

Her body turned in on itself, unfolding layer after layer of sensation until she reached a higher peak and leapt beyond it, with him, together. She felt sated, glutted, overflowing with bliss and love and the unbearable sweetness of her climax. Above her, Gary groaned in ecstasy and exhaustion.

Slowly, careful not to crush her, he lowered himself into her waiting arms. She hugged him tightly, and he dropped a tender kiss onto her lips.

"The after-dinner cordial." She guessed.

He grinned and kissed her again, a little less cordially. "You look pretty stuffed to me."

She refused to let his baiting bother her. "I'm not stuffed. Just...very full."

"Thank God for healthy appetites." She felt him soften and slide from her, leaving her feeling just a little less full but still very much in love. "I've been dreaming about making love with you from the minute I saw you in the jury room, that first day," he confessed, his smile waning. "But..." He sighed. "Wow. I never imagined it would be this good. I never knew it *could* be this good."

His words brought tears to her eyes. She could easily have praised him as highly—but that was because he was a sublime lover. The same could not be said for her. She'd scarcely touched him. She hadn't thought to curl her legs around his waist, or to guide him with her hands, or to do anything but lie on her back and let him have his magnificent way with her—after first humiliating herself by coming too soon. "I thought I was fumbling," she muttered.

He laughed out loud. "If that was fumbling, I'd hate to see you at your best. I think it would kill me."

"I wouldn't want to kill you," she said. "Especially after you've fed me so well."

"We fed each other," he remarked, mischief tweaking his smile back to life. "What's a boutique steak without the steak sauce? And enough heat to make the meat sizzle...."

She was blushing again, but she was long past caring. "You're terrible!" she scolded, pretending she was going to hit him.

His grin grew more roguish. "And those buns of yours are so tasty...."

"How would you know? You didn't taste them."

"The night is young." He eased off her, then rolled her onto her belly, ignoring her shrieks of laughter and protest. He planted a row of kisses the length of her spine, from top to bottom. By the time he was done, she wasn't laughing anymore. She was too turned on. She was hot and seething, impossibly hungry given the feast he'd just given her.

She rose onto her side. He looked aroused, too. She skimmed her hand down his body from his shoulder to his groin. He felt aroused. The laughter vanished from his eyes, replaced by a curiously helpless yearning as she closed her hand around his hardness and stroked him fully to life.

"If this does kill me," he whispered, circling her waist with his hands and lifting her until she was straddling his body, 'I'll die happy." With that, he pulled her down, and

Sophie happily succumbed once more to the erotic gluttony of loving Gary.

HE COULDN'T SLEEP.

Part of it was the noise. Even at 2:00 a.m., a muted cacophony of city sounds seeped into his consciousness: a distant siren, a sigh of tires against the pavement, a disembodied voice singing an old Beatles tune off-key, the lyrics garbled but loud. How could anyone live with such a constant din roiling the atmosphere?

He eased himself out from under the blanket, careful not to disturb Sophie, and tiptoed to the window. Peering out, he saw the cars—his own among them—lined up bumper to bumper along both sides of the block. Across the street, apartment buildings huddled close together, an occasional window lit from inside. Evidently Gary wasn't the only person suffering from insomnia.

Part of it was the city, yes. But part of it, he acknowledged as he let the curtain drop back across the glass, was the woman.

Turning, he gazed at her. She slept the way she made love: with abandon. Her hair spilled in a cascade of pale curls across her pillow. Her lips were pouted and her body stretched seductively under the blanket. He could trace the angles of her knees where the cover draped over her, the rise of her hip and slope of her waist. Unfortunately, the blanket didn't drape over all of her. It had slipped down to reveal the creamy swell of one breast, a sight so alluring, he felt himself get hard.

Again.

Cripes. He wasn't a kid anymore. He must have used up

his entire supply of hormones hours ago. His back was stiff, his legs, his neck—and one other part of his anatomy was implacably stiff, too.

He hadn't been exaggerating when he'd told Sophie he didn't know sex could be quite this spectacular. He and Meg had had a fine time of it, but that was so long ago, and when he'd lost her he had deliberately stopped thinking about their lovemaking because it had only made his grief worse.

Over the years he'd dated. He'd known women. He'd had his share of relationships. But none of those women had made him feel so...complete. Energized. Able to leap tall buildings in a single bound.

God help him, he could actually learn to enjoy spending sleepless nights in a city if Sophie was with him.

He crept back to the bed, determined not to rouse her. But when he slid under the blanket, it drooped lower to display both her breasts, small but firm and perfectly round, each one tipped with an exquisite pink nipple.

His mouth watered.

He needed to get some rest. If she woke up well rested and full of vigor, while he was a zombie from a lack of sleep, she was going to sway the jury back to Jocelyn Kramer's side. Which, in the grand scheme of things, no longer seemed to matter that much to Gary.

This was exactly why Sophie hadn't wanted them to get intimate before the end of the trial—she'd been afraid of losing her perspective during the deliberations. But now it seemed that Gary, not Sophie, was the one who was going to pay for their indulgence. Six hours from now, she was going to waltz into the jury room, fresh and invigorated, and he was going to stagger in, haggard and drained. And meanwhile, his principles would go forgotten.

Somewhere below his waist, his body told him principles weren't all that important.

Unable to resist, he inched the blanket down to Sophie's waist and took one nipple into his mouth. She sighed and stirred, but didn't awaken. He licked the flesh and nipped it until it swelled into a delectable point. She moaned softly, but her eyes remained shut.

Emboldened, he shoved the blanket lower, past her belly, past her hips to her knees. She murmured something—his name, perhaps—but didn't tell him to stop. He brushed his lips over her midriff, then nibbled down to her belly. She had the sexiest navel he'd ever seen. But then, everything about Sophie was incredibly sexy—particularly her utter lack of awareness about how sexy she was.

She murmured something again, a velvet-soft whisper that sounded more like assent than refusal. He urged her legs apart and kneeled between them. Cupping his hands around her hips, he bowed and pressed his mouth to her. She lurched, and he held her tighter.

Her body twisted beneath his mouth as he drank her in. Gary was drunk with the sensation of her coming apart against his lips. He slid his tongue deep and she moaned.

"Gary?" Her voice emerged broken and choked.

He couldn't exactly talk himself. She was still pulsing, still trembling as he lifted his head.

"Why did you do that?" she asked breathlessly.

"Because..." *Because you looked so beautiful, so vulnerable. Because I'm falling in love with you. Because I wanted to hear you moan*. "Because the blanket slipped down, and there you were."

She reached down and pulled him up beside her. "You scare me," she whispered.

"Really?" He wasn't sure she meant that as a compliment, but in a perverse way the comment appealed to him. "Why?"

"You're too good to be true."

Definitely a compliment. "I'm true, sweetheart."

"If you bragged about being good, you'd be right." She snuggled up against him, her body molding to his. "Too good to be true..." Her voice grew thick with drowsiness.

Within a minute, she was asleep. Gary closed his eyes, listening to her breathe, listening to a bus rumble down the main thoroughfare at the end of Sophie's street. Listening to his own rampaging heartbeat, and his own doubts and hopes and longings.

If this was too good to be true, he wanted it. He deserved it. Sophie deserved it, too.

They'd get through the trial, put it behind them and then spend the rest of their lives enjoying this too-good-to-be-true thing. That soothing thought was enough to lull him to sleep.

IF THE OTHER JURORS noticed that Gary was wearing the same clothing he'd had on yesterday, they didn't remark on it. If they had, Sophie wouldn't have minded. After last night, she couldn't care less what people thought about her and Gary. She was in love, she had every reason to believe her feelings were returned and as soon as this damned trial was over, she and Gary could concentrate on their relationship.

There were details to iron out, certainly. As a single father,

Gary had to be sensitive to his son's feelings—although if her one meeting with Tim was a fair indication, she didn't see major problems on that front. That Gary lived on a farm in the middle of nowhere was a bit more of a hurdle, but even that could be dealt with. Sophie was so besotted, she could imagine herself living in that charming old farmhouse, surrounded by trees and corn and dogs. The bucolic peace might make her crazy, but Gary's love would cure her insanity.

She could get her daily dose of city life commuting to the store. She'd have to buy a car, of course.... She'd have to join the legions of suburbanites who came into the city for their allotted eight hours, then headed for the hills as fast as their cars could carry them. It was always possible, of course, that she could lure Gary into the city after a hard day of farm labor. They could meet somewhere: at a café in the North End, at a snack bar at Faneuil Hall, at Fenway Park for hot dogs and baseball. She could prove to him that even though Boston and Cambridge weren't considered worthy of coverage in his odd little county newspaper, urban life had a great deal to offer.

But that could all be worked out later. As long as Gary felt for her what she felt for him, no problem was insurmountable. She would pledge him her love, and he would pledge his to her, and the rest would be a piece of cake.

She waltzed into the jury room, trying to remember the issues of the Kramer-McGuire trial. The humiliated bride, the heartless groom, the enormous sums of money lost...the precious clapboard chapel and the historic inn...

Would Gary be willing to marry her at that chapel? If he loved her enough, surely he would. She wouldn't spend tens of thousands of dollars on dresses and flowers, but they could exchange their vows in that lovely little chapel, couldn't they? With her family and his in attendance, maybe Tim standing up for Gary. She'd bet Tim would be willing to trade his obscene Get Naked And Party T-shirt for a real suit and tie for the occasion. Sophie would buy both Brett men ties. Gary's father, too, if hideous taste in ties was a family trait.

All four other jurors were already in the jury room when Sophie and Gary arrived, and they all appeared considerably more awake than Gary. She would have thought that farmers were used to rising with the sun—or perhaps with the crow of a rooster. If she married him, would she have to wake to a rooster's crow, too?

If she did, she did. Gary Brett was worth it.

Well, he had a valid reason to be sleepy that morning, she thought with a private smile as she crossed to the coffee machine to get a cup of coffee. She filled a cup for him, too, but when she turned around to hand it to him, she saw him chatting with Jack Reilly. He was doing his best to act normal, and she followed his lead. Setting the extra cup of coffee down beside the pot, she carried her own coffee to the table and took the vacant chair next to Phillip.

"This thing better be over today," he growled.

"If we put our minds to it, we'll reach a verdict," she assured him. A verdict was actually quite likely that morning. Gary was really the sole force for the opposition, after all. Louise could go either way—she'd already gone both ways—but now that Gary had spent a night in Sophie's arms, surely he could find it in his heart to soften his views. If he loved Sophie—and given his passion and sensitivity last night, she had to believe he loved her—he would at least try to see things from her perspective. And if he did, he would have to find for Jocelyn Kramer.

"Let us get started," Miss Prinz orated from the head of the table. Gary and the sandhog took their seats across the table from Sophie and Phillip, and Louise, munching on a doughnut that leaked confectioner's sugar down the front of her shirtwaist dress, took a seat on Gary's other side.

Miss Prinz gazed down the table as if she were a queen and the other jurors were her subjects. "I would like to presume you are all well rested," she said, her stare lingering just a bit too long on Gary in his rumpled shirt, with his rumpled hair and his rumpled, ugly tie. Her eagle-sharp gaze skidded across the table to Sophie, who felt her cheeks grow warm. Obviously, at least one person in the jury room had managed to put two and two together.

Sophie couldn't control her blushing, but she could control her pride. Nothing Miss Prinz could say or do, no glaring disapproval in her scowl, was going to make Sophie apologize for last night.

"We have several options before us," Miss Prinz went on. "We can continue to argue, or we can attempt to find a verdict we can all live with. I don't believe we have any great disagreement on the issues here. Even the plaintiff and the defendant have no real disagreement. Our deadlock is over nuances and morals—"

"It's over what kind of broad spends that much money on flowers," Jack Reilly blurted out.

Sophie bit her lip. Jack's comment implied that he had switched camps overnight.

"I would not choose to put it so crassly," Miss Prinz commented. "However, I think you've touched on the main point, Mr. Reilly."

"I have?" He beamed proudly, then leaned forward to look past Gary at Louise. "Where'd you get that doughnut? Did you have to pay for it yourself?"

Miss Prinz didn't give Louise a chance to answer. "The main point, it seems to me, is money. Mr. McGuire and Miss Kramer had an agreement. Mr. McGuire reneged on it. He owes Miss Kramer something. Does anyone wish to dispute this assessment?"

Sophie eyed Gary. He looked too tired to dispute anything. Yet the smile he sent her when his gaze met hers implied that he wouldn't be too tired to scoop Sophie up and haul her off to bed again, as he nearly had when she'd been rushing around that morning, trying to get ready for court. Instead of hauling her to bed, he'd hauled her into the shower. She'd warned him that they didn't have a minute to spare, that they had barely enough time to get dressed and down to the courthouse by eight o'clock, and he'd murmured something about how they both had to shower and why not save time by doubling up. If she wasn't mistaken, he had run the bar of soap over every inch of her body—although he'd concentrated more on some parts of her body than on others. They hadn't saved any time at all.

She was blushing again, damn it. And grinning like a woman madly in love.

The lack of debate encouraged Miss Prinz to continue. "So, we're all in agreement, then?"

"I do think there's a moral issue involved," Sophie said, surprising herself. "And while I hate to attach a price tag to morality, I think we need to consider the fact that a marriage was supposed to take place. And it didn't, because of Mr. McGuire. That's more than simply reneging on an agreement. When a woman gets treated that way, when her heart is broken so cruelly—"

"This isn't about your heartbreak," Gary interrupted. "Try to be objective, Sophie. This is about Jocelyn Kramer, not your run-in with that idiot who dumped you way back when."

If her cheeks had felt hot before, they felt cold now, the blood draining from them. She wasn't upset that Gary had dared to argue with her—even people wildly in love were allowed to bicker. Nor did she take exception to his tone, which was cool and reasonable.

What rattled her was that, after last night, after they'd been so close, shared so much, opened so fully to each other...she hadn't expected him to march into the jury room girded for battle. To bring up her debacle with Mitchell, even if everybody in the room knew about it, seemed...well, extreme. Gary was fighting her left, right and center over this stupid verdict.

As fatigued as he might be after last night, as romantically as he'd showered with her that morning, the moment he'd entered the jury room, he'd stopped being Sophie's lover and reverted to being a juror. A stubborn, pugnacious, victory-or-death juror.

If that was how he intended to behave, she'd fight back. If Gary wanted to be a juror, oh, yes, she'd be a juror, too. She'd give as good as she got. "This isn't about my own heartbreak," she said crisply, praying that her voice wouldn't crack. "It's about Jocelyn Kramer's. McGuire hoodwinked her. She wanted a wedding, and he promised her one. She wanted a marriage, and he'd promised her a marriage."

"That's exactly it!" Gary declared, pouncing on her statement. "She wanted a wedding and a marriage. It had nothing to do with McGuire."

"It had everything to do with him!"

"Like hell. Who says a marriage is the same thing as a relationship? You love someone, you make a commitment to that person and that's that. Weddings and marriages have nothing to do with it."

His sensible tone infuriated her, especially because what he was saying made no sense. "That's ridiculous! What do you think a marriage is? It's a commitment!"

"Not a particularly useful one, when you consider how easy it is to get a divorce. The commitment has to come from inside a person. It's nothing a minister can give you, or a priest, or a rabbi, or a justice of the peace. It has nothing to do with getting a marriage license at city hall. That's just paperwork. It's bureaucracy. It's gestures—sometimes grand gestures, sometimes empty gestures, but nothing more significant than that. A commitment is a completely different thing, and you don't need a fancy white chapel for that."

Sophie shook her head, amazed that Gary, of all people, could say such a thing. He was a father, a widower, a devoted family man. "You don't really believe that, Gary," she asserted. "If you did, you'd never have gotten married yourself."

"I never did get married," he said.

Her throat froze shut. He'd never gotten married? How could that be? He had a son! If he was prepared to lie about his family just to get the verdict he wanted, what kind of man was he? "I don't understand," she said, forcing out the words. "You told me your wife died—"

"I told you my son's mother died."

Her heart started pounding. She breathed slowly, afraid she might roar with fury, or maybe throw something. It was true: he'd told her his son's mother had died. Which meant he must have fathered Tim out of wedlock and, when Tim's mother passed away, gotten the kid dumped in his lap.

And she'd thought he was noble and honorable! She'd thought he was a decent, responsible family man!

"Marriage was never important to Tim's mother and me," he explained, his voice twice as scary for being so calm. "We loved each other and we made a commitment, and what we had was a hell of a lot better than most marriages I've seen. What kept us together wasn't a piece of paper, wasn't a contract, wasn't a few words recited at an altar. It was love. That was it. We had a son because we loved each other. We lived together because we loved each other, and if Meg hadn't died, we'd probably still be together. That's what relationships are all about. Not thousand-dollar dresses with pearls sewn on the front. Not bridesmaids and flowers and a sit-down dinner for two hundred people. We didn't need a stupid piece of paper."

Sophie's mouth flopped open, and she exerted herself to shut it. *A stupid piece of paper?* Was that truly what Gary thought a marriage was all about? Gary Brett, the farmer, the Norman Rockwell family man, chose not to marry the woman he loved because marriage was *a stupid piece of paper?* And he didn't *need* it? How could he not have married the woman he loved? How could he have had a son with her?

How could he act as if thousands of years of ritual and tradition were unnecessary?

People got married because they loved each other. Marriage meant more than she could describe in words. It meant for better or worse, in sickness and in health, as long as ye both shall live. It meant being declared a husband and wife, in the eyes of God and the law. Sophie intended to get married someday, to someone who understood just how sacred and valuable marriage was.

Obviously, that someone wasn't Gary. Not a man who had so little regard for *a stupid piece of paper*. Not a man who could belittle the most beautiful, romantic promise a loving couple could ever make.

She loved him. She'd dreamed of all kinds of things with him—growing closer, merging their lives, shaping a shared future. She'd dreamed of Gary waiting for her at the front of that beautiful chapel, and she would walk down the aisle to him, and take his hand, and wear his ring. She had actually believed such a thing could happen.

But it never would, not with Gary. And the realization hurt worse than anything any other man had ever done to her. This wound was deep, it was agonizing, and she couldn't imagine it would ever heal.

10

BY TEN-THIRTY, the jury was ready to issue its verdict to the court. They found in favor of Jocelyn Kramer, but limited the damages Ronald McGuire would have to pay to the actual expenses Jocelyn and her family had incurred—which admittedly added up to a lot of spare change. The jury decided not to require McGuire to pay Kramer's legal fees, since they felt the financial terms could have been negotiated in good faith, without resorting to courts and lawyers. That Jocelyn had decided to hire an attorney meant that she should be required to pay for that attorney.

It all seemed pretty cut-and-dried to Gary. The verdict was delivered, the judge pounded her gavel and the jury was dismissed.

All six of the elevators in the courthouse building were working, so the jurors didn't have to wait long for one to arrive and carry them downstairs. Less than ten minutes after the judge had thanked Gary and his colleagues for their service, he was outdoors, trying to ignore the chill of the overcast morning, and also trying to ignore Jack Reilly, who wanted Gary's input on whether he ought to take the whole day off and tell his foreman the jury hadn't reached a verdict until late in the day. "If I go back to the job site, they're going to put me to work," the sandhog complained. "If I stay away, they've still got to pay me—unless they find out we finished up early. But if they do find out, I could get my butt nailed to the wall. What do you think?"

"Go to work," Gary told him, his gaze trained on the building's main entrance.

People went in. People came out. People milled just inside the door and just outside it. But the one person he needed to see never appeared.

She must have left the court building ahead of him. Gary had seen her leave the jury room with Louise and head down the hall to the ladies' room. Figuring that she would return, he had loitered in the jury room, wasting time, listening to Jack Reilly ramble about the most effective way to shirk his job now that the trial was done. But Louise had come back from the ladies' room alone, and in answer to Gary's question, she'd reported that Sophie hadn't been with her.

He'd searched the corridor. He'd scrutinized the passengers entering and exiting the smoothly functioning elevators. Reluctantly, he'd reached the unhappy conclusion that Sophie had given him the slip.

Why? Just because he'd spoken the truth?

His body was still aching from last night—but not nearly as much as his mind, his soul, his gut. He wanted Sophie, wanted her insanely. He wanted her in every way there was to want a woman. But apparently she didn't care for the sort of man who thought the promises you made with your heart were more important than the promises you made in a chapel. She thought public proclamations were more valid than private commitments. She believed megabucks weddings were the true measure of love.

He was sure he could convince her otherwise, just as he'd convinced his fellow jurors that Jocelyn Kramer didn't have the right to milk Ronald McGuire's bank accounts just be-cause she was disappointed by the way things had worked out for her. But if Gary was ever going to convince Sophie, first he had to find her.

"Jack, it's been great, but I've got to go," he said, inter-rupting the sandhog before he could ruminate further on how much gold-bricking his jury duty was good for. With a wave, Gary turned and jogged down the block to the garage.

Maybe Sophie had gone home. He could catch her at her apartment, and talk to her, and kiss her...and prove to her that his philosophy of what made for a real relationship was a lot better than hers.

Reaching the garage, he raced up the stairs to the level where he'd parked. He climbed into his car, keenly aware of how empty it seemed without her in the seat beside him. Well, he'd have her with him soon enough, he swore. He'd convince her to see things his way. He'd explain to her that the partnership he'd had with Meg, while lacking the trap-pings of society's approval, was a hell of a lot stronger and closer than any legal marriage he'd ever known. Sophie was smart, and he was pretty sure she was feeling for him what he was feeling for her. Surely they could work this out. All he had to do was find her.

The drive to her apartment reminded him of one thing he hated about cities: traffic. Red lights thwarted him. Transit buses cut him off. Cabs weaving from lane to lane spurred homicidal urges in him. The entire city of Cambridge seemed to have formed a conspiracy to keep him from reach-ing her. He wanted to roll down his window and shout, "This is an emergency! Get out of my way!"

At last he reached her block—but naturally he couldn't

find a parking space. Leaving his car double-parked in front
of her building, he stormed up the front steps, entered the
foyer and punched the intercom button next to her name. No
response. He punched it again, then leaned on it until the tip
of his thumb was flattened.

Either she had stuffed putty into her ears so she wouldn't
hear her buzzer, or she wasn't home.

But where would she have gone? Her shop—the crafts
boutique. If only he could remember its name....

Damn. He squeezed his eyes shut, as if that would wring
this one misplaced memory from a dark corner of his mind.
She'd told him the name of the shop; it was in storage somewhere in his gray matter.

Simple something. Simple Simon? Simply...*Divine*. That
was it. Simply Divine.

He had no idea where the store was located, and he told
himself he shouldn't take the time right now to search the
city for it. Back in Stow he had work awaiting him. The farm
required his attention; Tim might appreciate a glimpse of his
father, too. And Pop probably hadn't remembered to feed
the dogs. They could be prowling the kitchen right now,
bumping into furniture and moping. Gary really had to get
home to take care of business.

He could phone Sophie that evening, once she'd calmed
down and the final deliberations of the jury faded from her
mind. The sun would set, and she would be lying all alone in
that nice, broad bed of hers, in the dark. And recalling the
previous night, she would be open to anything Gary might
say.

Going home was surely the logical thing to do. But Gary
wasn't feeling particularly logical. In fact, he was on edge,

his nerves unraveling by the minute. If he didn't find Sophie, he would disintegrate.

He left her building, got back into his car and set off in search of a telephone directory. The clerk at a neighborhood convenience store lent him her city phone book once he had proven his worth by purchasing two dollars' worth of chewing gum. He flipped frantically through the pages until he found a listing for Simply Divine. He jotted the address and phone number on a napkin, thanked the clerk and tossed the ten-pack of chewing gum in the trash bin on his way out the door.

Sophie's shop was located not far from Harvard Yard. Surrounded by bookstores, gourmet coffee emporiums and the like, the place exuded arty-highbrow style. The display window featured a woven blanket draped with casual precision over a wicker chair, and some odd-shaped ceramic bowls placed here and there.

He stared at the window display for a long minute, then mustered his courage and pushed open the door. The contrast between his life and Sophie's shouldn't matter. It *didn't* matter, he told himself. What mattered was that they had something special going for them, and given the chance, it could become a lot more special. If only Sophie could cut loose and lead with her heart.

The interior of the shop was as rarefied as the front window had led him to expect. Elegant ceramic pieces stood on tables around the room. Wind chimes tinkled in the breeze from the open door. Hand-beaded blouses and tapestried vests hung from brass coat trees along one wall. Along the opposite wall ran shelves filled with an assortment of bowls, painted dishes, planters and trays. Pop would call them dust collectors. They were a far cry from the beer mugs and ashtrays on the shelves of the Brett family's dining room hutch.

A painfully thin woman with spiky black hair and an anemic complexion approached him, smiling blandly. "Can I help you?"

"I'm looking for Sophie Wallace. Is she here?"

The woman's smile faded slightly, causing her cheekbones to press against her chalky skin. "She's busy right now. Perhaps I could help you instead. Are you looking for anything in particular?"

"Yes. I'm looking for Sophie in particular," he said, frustrated that he had to repeat himself but relieved that he'd succeeded in tracking Sophie down. "Is she here?"

The woman regarded him for a moment longer, evidently trying to decide whether he was a customer, a friend or a psychopathic murderer. She must have scratched the last possibility, because she relented and said, "Why don't you tell me your name, and I'll let her know you're here."

"Gary Brett."

The woman pivoted on her chic platform shoes and strode to a door at the back of the shop. Gary trailed her, and when she swung the door open he caught it before it could latch shut.

"You can't come back here," the woman protested.

"Watch me," Gary said pleasantly, pushing his way past her into the spacious storage area beyond the door. One half of the room contained metal shelves crammed with more elegant knickknacks, and the other was fashioned into a makeshift office, with a large L-shaped desk, several file cabinets and a computer setup. The woman seated at the desk, tapping the computer keyboard, looked frazzled, tired, but more gorgeous than ever.

She glanced up from the computer monitor and gave a little yelp of surprise.

"Thanks," Gary murmured to the black-haired woman. "I'll take it from here."

"Gary." Sophie snapped off the computer and shoved herself to her feet. He felt his breath catch as he regarded her, resplendent in her anger, her eyes shooting sparks of rage, her mouth pursed into a scowl that looked more like the beginnings of a kiss, at least in his admittedly biased opinion.

"Do you want me to call the police?" the skinny woman said helpfully.

"No thanks, Lynn. I can handle this. He's just one of the jurors from my trial."

The woman named Lynn eyed Gary suspiciously but backed out of the storage area, closing the door behind her.

Gary wasn't usually given to indignation, but this was a bit much. "*Just one of the jurors? Is that what I am?*"

Sophie had the good sense to avert her eyes. "I didn't want to go into it with Lynn," she explained, then found the courage to glare directly at him. "But you *are* my trial at the moment. What are you doing here?"

"What do you think I'm doing here?"

"I don't suppose you want to buy a bowl."

At the moment, he wanted to give her a good shake, in the hope it would make her come to her senses. Shaking her would do him about as much good as losing his temper, so he kept his cool. "What I'm doing here is trying to convince you not to run away from me. I'm nuts about you, Sophie. I want us to give this thing a go."

"What thing? An affair with no strings attached?" Her cheeks bloomed with color, but Gary knew her blushing was from anger, not embarrassment. "Forget it. I'm too old for going steady—and even that would probably be too much of an obligation to you."

He took a few deep breaths, like a diver about to swim for his life. "What I said in the jury room—"

"You fathered a child out of wedlock, Gary! Even having a son wasn't enough for you to make it legal!"

"What I said in the jury room was that the most important thing in a relationship was honesty. I meant that. I never lied to you, Sophie, and I never would. I never lied to Tim's mother, either. She saw things exactly as I did. We knew who we were and what we meant to each other. We didn't need the approval of the rest of the world. What we had was more than most married couples ever have. And it was fine with her."

"Well, I guess she was a better woman than me," Sophie said. Her gaze remained unwavering on him. The only outward sign of her distress was her fidgeting hands, pushing scraps of paper around on her desk. "I'm petty and superficial. I like artificial things like legal marriages."

"Even though half of them end in divorce? Even though lots of marriages include dishonesty? I've had friends who cheated on their wives, friends whose wives cheated on them, friends who were married but didn't even make an effort to understand each other. They had the blessings of society, Sophie, but they had lousy relationships."

"And you think all marriages are like that?"

"My parents' marriage was like that. I grew up watching two people who went through the motions because of a piece of paper. They were never happy together. The paper didn't make them love each other, any more than getting a divorce could have made them more separate than they already were. What counted was what they felt for each other—or didn't feel."

"I'm sorry, Gary. I didn't know your parents had a bad marriage." Her gaze softened for a moment, then grew stony again. "I guess you're carrying some scars from that. It's skewed your vision a bit."

"It didn't skew my vision," he said, not willing to have her psychoanalyze him. "It just taught me what relationships were really about. They're about talking, and arguing, and laughing, and sharing thoughts and dreams, and having sex the way we did all night long. That's what love is."

Her hands were fluttering so wildly, she knocked a folder onto the floor. She seemed grateful for the excuse to turn her back on him and duck under her desk to gather the scattered papers.

Gary circled the desk and joined her on the floor, scooping up pages of the file. In spite of the fury emanating from her in palpable waves, he treasured her nearness. He inhaled her familiar wildflower scent, and it turned him on. Her hair was close enough to touch, her mouth close enough to kiss.

He wanted to make love to her, right there on the floor. But he also wanted to stay alive, and given how angry she was, he decided not to tempt fate by reaching for her.

Still, he saw no reason for them to stand like combatants on opposite sides of her desk. Once all the papers were tucked inside the manila folder, he grasped her wrists to keep her from rising. Her fingers twitched, but she didn't break from him. One tiny tug and he could tumble her into his lap.

Again, he opted not to risk her wrath. "What is it that really bothers you about all this?" he asked. "I thought we were in agreement that once the trial was over, we could give this relationship a shot. I know you like the city and I like the sticks, but we can work around that. And if you don't want to deal with Tim, that's okay. He's my son, and I'd die for him, but that's no concern of yours. You don't have to sign on with him if you don't want to."

"I like Tim," she said, her voice thick and soft.

"Or my father. He's a bit cranky, I know. And he's not as sophisticated as you are. I guess I'm not, either."

"I like your father, too, Gary. I like your family. Including the dogs."

Gary permitted himself a tiny smile. "I don't know about you," he pressed ahead, "but last night was one of the best nights of my life. We've got a hell of a lot going for us there, Sophie. That kind of chemistry is a rare thing."

"I know." She lowered her eyes once more, leaving him to stare at her thick golden lashes. "Last night was...well, yes, it was one of the best nights of my life, too. And your family is wonderful. And the fact that you live on the far side of nowhere—"

"Now, wait a minute! Stow isn't—"

"It doesn't matter. None of that matters." She lifted her eyes to gaze at him. They shimmered with tears. "I've always dreamed of saying 'I do.'"

"Then say it. It's just two words. Say it to me. Say it in your heart."

She shook her head. Her hands relaxed and she wove her

fingers through his. A tear seeped through her lashes, but she batted her eyes, blinking it away. "I'm not a rebel like you. I want the ritual. I want a square old-fashioned wedding."

"That's all it is—a ritual. Totally meaningless."

"To you, maybe. To me it has meaning. I want to be the legal wife of the father of my children. I want to wear a gold ring on my left hand. I want to swear in front of a room full of witnesses that I'm taking this man as my husband. I want to shout it to the world."

"Why?"

"I can't explain why, any more than you can explain why you consider it meaningless. This is who I am, Gary. This is what I need. And you aren't the man who can give me what I need."

Gary exhaled. Obviously he wasn't the only honest person in the room. Sophie was speaking her heart, even though her honesty led her to reject what he offered. Several tears broke free and skittered down her cheeks, and she didn't bother to wipe them away. She just curled her fingers through his and gazed at him, her expression so rueful, just looking at her hurt him.

He *could* give her what she needed...if he were willing to toss aside his fervent belief that love and trust had nothing to do with legal documents. But it bothered him that she needed something so...well, *petty* and *artificial* were her words, but they worked for him.

It took him a moment to realize that she was trying to wriggle her hands free. Reluctantly he loosened his hold on her, understanding that he had to let her go in every way. He couldn't give her what she needed. She had said it as plainly, as honestly, as she could.

He shoved himself to his feet, then cupped his hands around her elbows to help her up. As soon as she was standing, he released her and bent back down to pick up the file. He set it on the desk, then shoved his hands into his pockets to prevent himself from gathering her into his arms and kissing her until she changed her mind. Sophie wasn't a juror anymore. He had no right to try to make her see things his way.

He told himself it didn't matter. If she was so hung up on stuff that he considered at best irrelevant, then she probably couldn't give him what he needed, either.

A plaintive voice inside him argued that all he needed was her mind and her musical laughter and her sweet, hot body wrapped around him—and no one but Sophie could answer his needs. But he knew what made a long-term partnership work, and it wasn't just sex and laughter. It was shared values. It was viewing the world in pretty much the same way.

Sophie had already written him off. No shared values and world views there. She was half the distance to becoming another Jocelyn Kramer, weeping because she wanted a picture-book wedding. Not a relationship, not a lover willing to etch promises into his heart for her, but a wedding.

"Well," he said, trying not to let his disappointment show, "I've got an orchard in need of watering, and a couple of stupid dogs in need of food. I guess I'll be on my way."

She said nothing. Tears continued to spill down her cheeks, but she wouldn't sob, wouldn't close her eyes, wouldn't look away. He half hoped she would beg him to stay, agree to give his way a chance, swear that Tim was the greatest son in the world regardless of his parents' iconoclastic take on things. But she wouldn't. She was just another Jocelyn, surrounded by fine glass and pottery, in love with ceremony rather than soul.

He turned and strode out of the storage area, thinking that if he never got called for jury duty again, it would be too soon.

WHY WAS IT THAT SHE COULD have endured getting shafted by Mitchell without shedding a single tear, yet watching Gary stalk out of the back room of Simply Divine reduced her to a human version of Niagara Falls? For Mitchell, she'd rearranged her entire life. For Gary, all she'd done was fall in love.

If only she were a little more clearheaded. If only having Gary so close to her didn't fill her heart with a million dreams that could never come true. If only she could have agreed to continue seeing him on his terms, which would have given her the opportunity to bring him around to *her* terms, her perspective, her faith that marriage was what adults did when they loved each other and wanted to make a life together....

But she'd been afraid to try. She'd been afraid that if she continued to see him, she would only fall more and more deeply in love with him—until it was too late to draw back. And then, if she failed to convince him that she wanted to be his wife, not just some sort of common-law arrangement but the real thing, the whole nine yards, the vows at the altar...

She wouldn't have been able to bear it.

The irony was, she'd never seen herself as one of those grasping, desperate, marriage-fixated women. Her feelings for Gary weren't an outgrowth of her desire to be wed. They were about Gary and Gary alone.

But that didn't mean she couldn't want to be married, too. Not just married, but married to the man she loved.

Which happened, alas, to be Gary.

The door inched open and Lynn peeked around the edge. "Are you all right?"

"That depends on your definition of 'all right,'" Sophie quipped, hearing her voice waver as she yanked open a desk drawer and rummaged inside for the box of tissues she kept there. She dabbed at her eyes and blew her nose.

Lynn glanced over her shoulder, then pushed the door open wider and stepped into the storage area. "Who was that guy?"

"I told you—a juror."

"And he made you cry?"

"I'm not really crying," Sophie fibbed, dabbing her eyes again and hoping they wouldn't overflow.

"I could have him shot for you," Lynn suggested with admirable loyalty. "I don't like men who make my friends cry."

Sophie grinned through her misery. "Don't shoot him," she said. "He's got too many dependents." And he hadn't bothered to marry the woman who'd given birth to his most important dependent. He hadn't been able to see his way clear to marrying his son's mother.

Then again, his son's mother hadn't seemed to care.

"What happened on that jury, anyway?" Lynn asked.

"We hedged. We came up with a middle-of-the-road verdict. We found for the plaintiff but didn't give her everything she was asking for. And now it's done. It's history. I don't want to think about it anymore, Lynn. I just want to get these inventory lists updated."

Unpersuaded, Lynn crossed the room to the desk. "I still think maybe I ought to shoot that guy. What was he doing here, if the trial is over?"

"He was asking me..." She faltered, unsure of exactly what he'd been asking her. To be his woman? To go out on dates? To go to bed with him?

He wanted much more than sex from her, she knew. And he was willing to give much more. She actually believed that in his own mule-headed way he loved her—more than Mitchell had, more than any other man ever had.

"He was asking me to give him my heart, but not my hand," she finally answered Lynn.

"Scum," Lynn condemned him. "I'll have him shot."

"Don't bother. Just find out if that friend of yours—the banker fellow with the house on Martha's Vineyard—might still be interested in getting together with me."

"I'll check," Lynn promised. "Although I can't guarantee he won't turn out to be scum, too. They all are, you know."

Perhaps most men were. But Sophie couldn't shake the conviction that she would have an easier time of it if she stuck with scum she didn't love. How much damage could a man she didn't love do? How badly could he hurt her?

Nowhere near as badly as Gary Brett could.

GARY MUST HAVE HURT HER brutally, Sophie realized a week later.

She had gone on her blind date with the banker, and it had been pleasantly boring. He hadn't expressed a desire to see her again, and she'd been relieved. She didn't want to date just to date. She wanted to fall in love.

But she'd already done that. And she couldn't seem to recover from it.

The week after the trial had to be the longest of her life. The days dragged on, one after another, like prisoners on a forced march. She pulled herself through each day as if she were carrying the weight of the world's tragedies on her back. She was too listless to eat, too weary to sleep. She rushed through her showers, unable to wash away her memories of the shower she had taken with Gary.

It shouldn't be this painful, she told herself as hour after hour passed without him in it. It shouldn't be agony to arise from bed each morning, aware that she was not going to see him. It shouldn't be torture to go to bed each night, aware that he would never again be a part of her life.

She shouldn't be so in love with him, damn it.

She could think of one solution to her sorrow: telephone him and tell him she was willing to accept a relationship with him on his terms. But she hadn't given in to him on the fight for jury foreman, and she hadn't given in to him on the verdict. She certainly couldn't give in to him when it came to something as essential as a legal marriage.

If he loved her as much as she loved him, he would be the one to give in. Obviously he didn't love her enough.

Still, she spent too much time staring at her telephone each evening, wishing it would ring. She spent too much energy gazing toward the door of Simply Divine each time it opened, hoping Gary would enter, and sinking into a funk when the customer turned out to be someone else. She spent too much emotion trying to find an excuse to call him, to relent, to agree to try love his way.

But he didn't telephone. He didn't come to the store. And his refusal to contact her justified her decision to end their relationship while she still could.

It didn't make her happy. But the longer he stayed away, the wiser she felt. Sadder, but wiser.

By the time the call she was waiting for came, the longest week in her life had multiplied by two, and she was doubly sad and not feeling all that wise. It was a warm, breezy Friday afternoon, and she was arguing with a weaver whose wall hangings she sold. The weaver fancied herself a sensitive artiste, and she contended that Sophie ought to be charging twice as much for the wall hangings, because each one was an original, and if people were willing to pay one hundred dollars for them, surely they'd pay two hundred. Sophie was trying patiently to explain the realities of the crafts market to the weaver when the phone rang.

Fortunately, Lynn was with another customer, providing Sophie with an excuse to escape the weaver and answer the phone.

"Sophie?"

She'd been praying for this call, yearning for it. But the voice on the other end didn't sound romantic, or contrite, or heavy with passion. It sounded taut and hoarse and edged in panic. "Gary?"

"Oh, God, Sophie—I need you."

Instinctively her heart raced with worry. "Where are you? What happened?"

"I'm at Mass General Hospital. It's Tim, Sophie. He's been hurt, and I..." Gary's voice broke. "I need you."

11

THE DAY HAD STARTED out as well as could be expected, given that yet again, Gary woke up from a dream of Sophie to find himself alone in bed. Every day for the past two weeks had started like that, with him awakening to a feeling of desolation mingled with resentment.

Why couldn't she be open-minded? Why couldn't she understand that love and marriage did *not* necessarily go together, and that the essential element was love? Why couldn't she be a little more like Gary?

The answers didn't matter. He was simply going to have to accept the situation, which was that the most exciting, exasperating, sexually magnificent and intellectually challenging woman in the Middlesex County jury pool was never going to see things his way.

He'd arisen that morning, alone and glum about it as usual, and stomped downstairs to let out the dogs and prepare a pot of coffee. He'd grumbled at Tim, buried his nose in the newspaper when his father had joined him in the kitchen and then slammed out of the house to unlock the retail stand for the cleaning service he'd hired to prepare the place for the upcoming season. He'd filled the tractor with gasoline and turned the corn acreage. And all the while he'd felt alternately sorry for himself, angry at Sophie and royally ticked off at his own obstinacy.

Did he love Sophie enough to give her the wedding of her fantasies? Was he willing to invest time in a relationship with her on the chance that it might come down to that?

His only respite from constant, gnawing thoughts of her were Tim's baseball games. Tim was scheduled to play a home game that afternoon, and Gary counted the minutes until he could head off for the ball field behind the high school and forget about Sophie for a couple of hours. She was a part of him, a constant, aching, implacable part—but when Tim was playing baseball, Gary could tune out the pain for a while. He could focus on his son.

The sky was a cloudless sheet of blue, stretching gloriously above the field. The scent of popcorn and pizza wafted to him from the Booster Club's snack bar. The boys on the field ran and swung their bats, caught and threw balls with adolescent bravado.

Tim looked even taller than usual in his uniform, and his hair hung in tufts below the edge of his batting helmet as he sauntered to the plate for his first at-bat. He took a few warm-up swings; his stance was loose. He was clearly the most handsome, most talented, most graceful boy on the field—as far as Gary was concerned, anyway. Other parents might favor their own sons. But Gary, with all the abundant objectivity of a doting father, knew his son was better than anyone else out there.

And then the world changed. The pitcher threw a wild pitch that slammed into Tim's head, cracking his helmet and jerking his neck back. Tim crumpled, his limbs folding under him as he slumped to the ground.

Gary wasn't sure how many people he shoved aside in his charge down the bleachers to the field. Someone touched his shoulder, someone shouted his name. But he just barreled down the benches, seeing nothing but Tim lying on the base path beside home plate.

It seemed to take forever to reach the dugout. An umpire grabbed his arm and held him back as his coach and teammates huddled around Tim.

"That's my son!" Gary bellowed, yanking his arm free of the umpire's grip. "That's my son!"

Someone with a cellular phone dialed the police emergency number. Someone ran into the school building to get the nurse. Gary pushed past people, elbowing his way through the huddle to Tim's side.

Oh, God. He looked so pale. And he was so horribly still.

Soon, emergency medical technicians arrived and were fastening a brace around Tim's neck to immobilize it. A teammate was easing the bat out of Tim's hand. The coach was murmuring in Gary's ear that everything was going to be all right—and Gary's furious impulse to punch the coach in the mouth for saying that when it might not be true.

One of the medical technicians rose from the stretcher on which Tim was being strapped. He conferred with the coach for a minute, then approached Gary. "You're the father?" he asked.

Gary nodded numbly.

"We're going to Medevac him to Mass General," the technician said. "They're better equipped to handle a head injury there than any of the local hospitals."

"How could there be a head injury?" Gary demanded. "He was wearing a helmet!"

"Lucky thing he was. He'd be dead otherwise. Why don't

you follow in your car? We'll fly him ahead and get him scanned."

Scanned. Head injury. The words echoed in Gary's mind. They were going to fly his son in a helicopter to Massachusetts General Hospital because that huge medical facility was better equipped to *scan* Tim's *head injury.*

Oh, God. Gary couldn't bear it. He couldn't.

He didn't have much choice, though. He sat on the grass next to Tim, holding his hand. Gary whispered to Tim but got no response. *Head injury,* he thought, fear rising into his throat, practically choking him. *Head injury.* Beside Tim lay the cracked batting helmet, a visible testament to the force of the pitcher's throw.

Eventually the helicopter arrived, landing on the adjacent football field, and the technicians carried Tim away on a stretcher. Gary would have liked to fly with him, but then he wouldn't have his car if he needed it. And perhaps it was just as well that he would have a chance to collect himself before he reached the hospital.

Even though he broke the speed limit the entire way, it was the longest drive he'd ever taken. Yet he did use the time to calm down, to unclutter his brain and figure out what he was going to do once he got to Mass General.

Call Sophie, he thought.

He pressed harder on the gas pedal, as if speed alone could push that idea out of his head. Surely he ought to call Pop first. And then he ought to discuss Tim's condition with the doctors and wait patiently while they scanned him. Gary was going to stay cool, trust medical science and hang on to his optimism.

No. He couldn't remain optimistic, he couldn't stay cool. He couldn't be patient while his son had a *head injury*.

He needed Sophie. His need wasn't rational, but that didn't matter. His heart overruled his head, and his heart was desperate for her. He needed her confidence, her certainty. He needed her strength. He needed someone he could trust to put him back together if he fell apart.

The scenery blurred past him as his car sped along. Trees budding with leaves threw shadows across the windshield. Gary drove on, reciting to himself what he would do: Call Sophie. Call Sophie.

"No," he said aloud. "You'll call Pop, and you'll talk to the doctor. Everything will be fine. The coach said…the emergency medical technician said…" *Sophie. Call Sophie.*

By the time he reached the emergency room of the huge hospital complex, Tim had already been transferred to radiology for a brain scan. A receptionist asked Gary a bunch of dreary questions about his insurance and entered his answers into a computer. He asked if he could see the doctors who were taking care of Tim, but the clerk explained that it would do Tim more good to have those doctors with *him* instead of with his distraught father. "I'm sure they're doing everything they can for your son," she said sympathetically.

Her words sounded ominous to Gary. He swallowed and rummaged in his pocket for loose change. "Is there a public phone I could use?"

She directed him to a quiet alcove off the waiting area. Gary walked to the bank of phones, called Directory Assistance and got the telephone number for Simply Divine. He dialed, listened as the phone rang on the other end, jiggled his foot impatiently, drummed his fingers against the plastic surface of the phone box, chewed on his lip and fought against the urge to scream.

"Simply Divine. May I help you?" her voice sang through the line.

His muscles unclenched, and he sagged against the wall. Just this electronic connection to her, courtesy of Ma Bell, was enough to console him. "Sophie?" he rasped.

"Gary?" She sounded startled, and wary.

"Oh, God, Sophie—I need you."

She hesitated, apparently trying to decide whether he was worth rescuing. "Where are you?" she asked. "What happened?"

"I'm at Mass General Hospital. It's Tim, Sophie. He's been hurt, and I..." Gary's voice broke. "I need you."

There was no hesitation anymore. "I'll be right there. Where will I find you?"

"In the emergency room waiting area." Gratitude welled up in him, mixing with his dread, making him need her even more. "Sophie, I—"

"Hush. Sit tight, Gary. I'm on my way." The line went dead.

I'm on my way. Those four words resonated inside him, eroding the sharp edges of his fear. Her melodious voice soothed him like cool, crystalline water bathing a raw wound. *I'm on my way.* He just might survive the next few minutes after all.

Inhaling deeply, he inserted some more coins into the slot and dialed his home number. After four rings, the answering machine clicked on. Pop must have gone out to the retail stand to help the cleaning crew. Or he'd driven to Concord to visit his sweetheart. Or gone to the supermarket. Or—God forbid—headed over to the ball field to catch the last half of the game.

"Pop," Gary said into the mouthpiece, "I'm calling to let you know Tim got hurt during the game. We came to the hospital to have him looked at. As soon as I have a better idea of what's going on, I'll call again." It was a lousy way to inform his father, but what else could he do? At least he hadn't gone into detail about the critical nature of Tim's injury. He also hadn't mentioned which hospital he was calling from. The last thing he needed right now was for his father to hop into his truck and drive to Boston. Gary could barely handle his own unraveling nerves right now. He certainly couldn't deal with his father.

He walked back to the admissions desk. "Any word yet?" he asked the receptionist.

Her smile seemed too practiced to be genuine. "Please relax, Mr. Brett. Why don't you go get a cup of coffee? It will probably be a while before the doctors can report on your son's condition."

He couldn't go for coffee, not with Sophie on her way. He had to wait for her, exactly where he was. She'd told him to sit tight.

Sitting was out of the question. He was too agitated, too tense. He paced the waiting area, picked up a magazine, put it down, paced some more. At the sound of an elevator door sliding open, he flinched. The doctors who emerged bounded past him, and he resumed pacing. A middle-aged man pushed an elderly woman in a wheelchair through the waiting room. An orderly wheeled an empty gurney down the hall.

He glanced at the clock and cringed. Nearly thirty minutes

had passed since he'd arrived—which meant close to an hour since Tim had been brought in on the medical helicopter. What were they doing to him? When was someone going to tell Gary what was going on? How was he going to bear up until they did?

Why had Tim's helmet cracked? Was it defective? Was the ball too hard? Why had Gary let Tim play baseball, anyway? Why hadn't he locked Tim up in the house—in a cozy, padded room where Tim would never, ever get hurt?

I'm on my way. Sophie's voice filled his memory with its sweet reassurance. Why had he fought with her? Why had they disagreed? They'd somehow managed to find a compromise in that damned Kramer-McGuire verdict. Why couldn't they have found one in their relationship?

"Gary?"

At first he thought he'd dreamed her voice, because he was so anxious to hear it. He turned around slowly, expecting nothing. And there stood Sophie, the only person he could imagine getting him through this disaster.

She looked windblown, her hair more disheveled than usual, the collar of her blouse crooked underneath the neck band of a brightly colored cardigan. Her arms opened, and he practically hurled himself into them. God, she felt so good, so solid, so secure. For the first time since Tim's legs had buckled under him at the baseball field, Gary felt hopeful.

He clung to her, reveling in her familiar scent, her familiar strength, the warmth of her embrace. He would have clung to her forever, but she gently loosened her hold and eased back from him. "What happened?" she asked, her eyes bright with concern.

"Tim was hit by a wild pitch. His batting helmet cracked and he was knocked unconscious. It was a head injury. A head injury," he repeated, because the words were so dire, he couldn't quite accept the reality of them.

"Oh, Gary." She gathered him to herself for another hug, evidently aware that he needed one. Then she led him to a bench along one wall and sat with him. She closed her hands around his. Her palms were smooth and cool.

Neither of them spoke for a minute. "What's happening now?" she finally asked.

"I don't know. He's getting a brain scan." Gary closed his eyes and shook his head. It all seemed unreal for him. Everything about the past hour of his life seemed unreal—except for Sophie's hands. Except for her quiet, consoling touch.

"Will they let you see him?"

"Not now. The lady over there—" he motioned with his head toward the clerk at the admissions desk "—told me it'll be a while before they know how bad the injury is. He just..." Closing his eyes again, he visualized the scene: his son so lanky and proud, swinging his bat into position above his right shoulder, bracing himself for the pitch. Had the sun been so bright and warm? Had the field looked so green and well-groomed? "I'm sorry," he said abruptly. "I know I'm going nuts here. I shouldn't have dragged you into it."

"Oh, Gary, I'm so glad you did." She tightened her hands around his. "This isn't something you should go through alone."

"I'm afraid of losing Tim..." His voice faltered, and he fell silent.

"You're not going to lose Tim."

"How do you know that?"

"Why assume the worst? He's a strong boy, and he was wearing the helmet. If it cracked, it must have absorbed a lot of the impact. I'm sure he'll be all right."

Her optimism was exactly what he needed. They continued to sit on the bench, holding hands, Gary trying to absorb her positive attitude through his fingertips. Nurses strolled past, orderlies pushed carts of drugs up and down the hall, and then the elevator door opened again and an authoritative-looking man sauntered over. "Mr. Brett?" he asked.

Gary lurched to his feet, trying unsuccessfully to quell his pounding heart. "Yes?"

"I'm Dr. Stuart Goldman. I'm a neurologist here on the staff."

Gary reluctantly let go of Sophie so he could shake the doctor's hand. She rose to her feet, too, and touched her hand to Gary's elbow, as if she knew how profoundly he needed that physical connection to her.

"Your son is a very lucky boy," Dr. Goldman said.

The words took a moment to sink in, and when they did, Gary had all he could do not to start blubbering with tears of relief. "How is he? Can I see him?"

"You can see him in a few minutes. He's suffered a concussion, and we'd like to admit him overnight for observation."

"But he's not going to be—crippled or anything? He's not going to die?"

"No," Dr. Goldman said with such certitude, Gary had to believe him. "Now, I'd like to have him transferred to ICU for the night. You'll have to fill out some forms—what's life without bureaucracy, right? I'm going to get your son settled, and then we'll bring you upstairs to see him." The doc-

tor gestured toward the reception desk where the receptionist sat at her computer.

Gary thanked the doctor and walked over to the desk, Sophie less than a step behind him. The receptionist ushered
him through another interrogation, entering vast quantities
of data into her computer and then printing out scads of paper for Gary to sign. He signed everything eagerly, joyfully,
trembling with gratitude that Tim wasn't going to die. He
signed, and signed again, signed on this line and that, next to
every X the clerk inked onto every page. By the time he was
done signing forms, a nurse approached and announced that
she would bring Gary to see Tim.

"Just a short visit," she warned as she led him and Sophie
into the elevator. "I think you need to see him more than he
needs to see you. He's very tired."

Numb with relief, Gary simply took Sophie's hand in his
once more, and held on tight.

The elevator opened onto a well-lit corridor, and the nurse
escorted them to an intensive-care unit. Small, partitioned
rooms surrounded the central nurse's station. At one room,
the nurse paused, checked the clipboard hanging next to the
door and then eased the door open. "Remember," she whispered, "just a few minutes."

Gary didn't suppose it would take longer than a few
minutes to tell Tim he loved him. He entered the small,
dimly lit cubicle, tugging Sophie in behind him. Beyond a
partially drawn curtain he found Tim stretched out in a mas-
sive hospital bed, a thick swatch of gauze bandaging his
forehead above his left eyebrow. His eyes were closed, but
his color had returned a bit. Even in a hospital bed, surrounded by monitors and hooked up to an IV drip, he looked

much healthier than he'd looked lying ashen and motionless on the baseball field less than two hours ago.

"Tim?" Gary whispered.

Tim opened his right eye. "Dad," he croaked, and then his eye opened wider. "Hey, Sophie!"

"Hi, Tim," she said, sounding much more serene than Gary. "How are you feeling?"

"Lousy," Tim said, then laughed weakly. "I should've gotten the base."

Sophie frowned for a moment, then nodded. "That's that rule you explained to me," she recalled. "If you get hit by a pitch, you're allowed to walk to first base."

Gary stared at her, amazed and touched that she remembered the technical baseball rules Tim had told her the night she'd come for dinner. That she had paid attention and remembered made him adore her.

He turned back to his son. Tim was wearing a cotton hospital gown. Gary wondered where his son's uniform was, whether the doctors had cut it off him in a mad rush to save his life. "Does it hurt? Your head, I mean."

"Yeah." Tim swallowed. "They said I was in a helicopter."

"Yes."

"I don't remember."

"That's all right."

"It was my first time in a helicopter, and, like, I don't even remember."

"Maybe you'll get another chance to ride in one someday. I hope to God it's not a Medevac, though."

"Yeah." Tim swallowed again. He looked thin in the baggy cotton nightshirt. "Did we win?"

Gary knew he was asking about the ball game. But he

didn't give a damn about who won. All that mattered was that his son was alive, able to see, able to hear, able to recognize people, able to speak. "Yes," he murmured. "We won."

"Good." Tim nestled deeper into the pillow and closed his eyes.

Gary took that as his sign to leave. "I'll be back later," he promised, patting Tim on the shoulder. In his condition, Tim wouldn't have the strength to protest paternal gestures of affection. "I love you, Tim."

He and Sophie left the small room, stopped at the nurses' station to inquire about visiting hours and then headed back to the elevator. Not until they were in it did she speak. "He seems okay."

Gary gazed about the elevator. It was slick and sterile, gliding smoothly down the shaft in a way the elevators at the courthouse never had. He recalled the trip he'd taken with Sophie when the elevator had stalled and the lights had gone out—and another light had gone on inside him, a light of passion and yearning unlike anything he'd ever felt before.

He missed her. Even with her standing just inches from him, her eyes wide and luminous, and her mouth curved in a half smile, he missed her. He missed her body, her mind, her spirit. He missed the magic that sparked between them whenever she was near. He missed knowing that if he reached for her she would be there, always.

"Do you have time for a cup of coffee?" he asked, wishing he could tell her how much he missed her. He couldn't, though. If he did, she would lapse into her blather about fancy weddings and public vows, everything he had rejected all his life.

"Sure," she answered, then turned from him and watched the blinking lights counting down the floors.

On the ground floor, they asked a clerk where they might find a snack bar. She gave them directions to a small commissary. The room was practically empty. Evidently no one wanted to eat anything this close to dinnertime.

Gary purchased two cups of coffee and carried them to a corner table. He helped her into a chair, then sat facing her across the narrow table. She blew the steam off the surface of her coffee and sipped. When her eyes met his over the rim of the cup, her gaze grew wistful.

He felt as wistful as she looked. It had all started with a cup of coffee, he recalled. That first morning of jury duty, he had bought her a cup of coffee, cream-no-sugar, and he'd almost lost her in the time it took to bring it back upstairs from the first-floor cafeteria.

He hadn't lost her then, though. He hadn't lost her due to bad timing or fickle fate. He'd lost her because of his stupid, stubborn principles.

"Tim really did seem okay," she observed, her voice velvet soft and gentle. "He recognized me right away, and he only met me once. He knew my name—"

"It's not as if I bring a woman home to dinner every day," Gary admitted. "Of course he would recognize you. You aren't easy to forget." It was a corny thing to say, but he was only speaking the truth.

She blushed. He missed her blush, too, he realized. He missed the way the delicate pink infused her cheeks. He missed the way it infused her entire body when they made love. "Anyway," she said, steering the conversation away from herself, "I think it's a good idea to have him spend the night here at the hospital, just in case. With a concussion, it pays to err on the side of caution. I'm sure he'll be released in a day or two."

"I don't like leaving him all alone here. I wonder if they'll let me spend the night. Some hospitals offer rooms to parents of sick kids, don't they?"

"I think that's for parents of young children. Not teenagers."

"Then I'll get a room in town," he decided. "There's probably a hotel not far from here. I don't want to have to drive back and forth from Stow. I'm enough of a wreck without having a forty-five-minute trip between me and my son."

"You can stay at my place," Sophie blurted out, then blushed again.

This was a different blush. Not a blush of embarrassment or chagrin, not a blush of sexual desire, but a blush of recognition that she'd just broken a promise to herself. He could guess what she'd promised: not to let him get too close. Not to let herself fall for a man who couldn't give her the proper, formal marriage she desired.

He contemplated her invitation. She hadn't told him he could spend the night in her bed, but sex wasn't what this was about. It was about her opening her home to him because he needed her. She had come running when he'd called, and she had stood by him, and she'd eased his torment and asked for nothing in return. She had refused to shut herself off from him when that would be her smartest, safest course. She'd come because he'd called, because he'd needed her so very much.

Before he could stop himself, he said, "Marry me."

She almost dropped her cup. With trembling hands, she placed it carefully into its saucer and glared at him. "What?"

"Marry me."

"Gary." She folded her hands and pursed her lips. "You're upset. You don't know what you're saying. You don't mean it."

"I'm not the one who got beaned with a baseball, Sophie. I know exactly what I'm saying, and I do mean it."

"You don't believe in marriage," she reminded him.

He let loose with a rousing laugh. Partly it was the release of all the tension he'd had knotted up inside him over Tim. But mostly it was a reluctant, helpless acknowledgment of what love could make a man do. "Do you realize that I've spent the last God-knows-how-long signing my name on every dotted line in this hospital? I didn't even stop to think about it. There were contracts and forms and insurance documents—official papers—and the hospital wanted them signed. And I signed them, because if I didn't, they might not have treated Tim."

Sophie frowned. Her hands had steadied themselves. She circled one finger around her cup, scrutinizing him, obviously perplexed. "What does that have to do with us?"

"I didn't care what the damned papers said," he explained. "I didn't think twice about it. All that mattered was getting Tim treated."

"So?"

"So, all that matters between you and me is that I want you in my life. And if signing a piece of paper on a dotted line is what it'll take for me to get what I want, then what the hell am I fighting it for? Show me the paper you want me to sign, Sophie. I'll sign it."

Her frown deepened. It dawned on him that this wasn't the romantic proposal she must have been fantasizing about all her life.

"Should I get down on one knee?" he asked belatedly.

"No. I don't want you to marry me because it'll get you what you want. That sounds so crass."

"I want you," he said bluntly. "I need you. I love you. What's crass about it?"

She seemed stumped. "I'm a city person," she pointed out.

"We can work on that." He leaned forward and captured her restless hand in his. "I'm willing to sign a marriage certificate. I'm willing to go legal for you. That's a bigger leap than your giving up Cambridge for the farm. Can't you meet me halfway?"

Her smile shimmered, its warmth coursing through him. "Well, we can't live in Cambridge. Your dogs would destroy my apartment, and we can't have that," she said. "I suppose I could get used to the farm, if I really had to."

"You have to," he declared, just so they could get down to the nitty-gritty. "Will you marry me?" This time his voice was low, earnest, husky with emotion. She could still say no, and if she did...if she turned him down...

"Yes," she said. "Yes, I'll marry you."

Now that she'd committed, a tremor of panic skimmed down his back. Gary Brett, *married?* Going through the rigmarole, the mumbo-jumbo, the empty rituals and stuffy traditions? He was thirty-seven years old, a father, a former Middlesex County juror—and he'd never before been married.

"We don't have to do it in that fancy white chapel, do

we?" he asked warily. "With tuxedos and thousand-dollar dresses?"

She smiled and shook her head. "We can do it in a judge's chambers, if you'd like. We can do it in City Hall. Just as long as you understand that it means you'll love, honor and cherish me for all your life."

"I'd do that even without the marriage," he vowed. He stood and pulled gently on her hand, and she rose from her chair and moved around the table to meet him. He wrapped her in a possessive hug. "In my mind," he murmured, "we could love, honor and cherish each other no matter what papers we signed. We're already there, Sophie. But if you want the paper, you've got it. Just don't ever leave me."

"I have what I want," she insisted, gazing up at him with glistening eyes. "Not ever leaving you is exactly what I want."

He bowed and kissed her. He didn't care if anyone entered the cafeteria, if anyone witnessed their passion. He didn't care if anyone wanted to tap into the joy he felt, holding his woman in his arms and swearing his love. That was what a marriage was, wasn't it? A public declaration of love, a sharing of joy.

This was Gary's joy. And if the world wanted to witness it, he didn't mind at all.

COMING NEXT MONTH

#758 BEAUTY & THE BEASTS • Janice Kay Johnson
Veterinarian Dr. Eric Bergstrom is interested in a new
woman. A *beautiful* woman. He's volunteered his services at
the local cat shelter she's involved with. He's even adopted
one of the shelter's cats. But he still can't manage to get
Madeline to go out with him. That's bad enough. Then Eric's
twelve-year-old son comes to town, making it clear that he
resents "having" to spend the summer with his father. Well,
at least Eric's new cat loves him....

#759 IN THE ARMS OF THE LAW • Anne Marie Duquette
Home on the Ranch
Morgan Bodine is part-owner of the Silver Dollar Ranch;
he's also the acting sheriff in Tombstone, Arizona.
Jasentha Cliffwalker is a biologist studying bats on Bodine
property. Morgan and Jaz loved each other years ago, but it
was a love they weren't ready for. *Are they ready now?*
They'll find out when a stranger comes to Tombstone,
threatening everything they value most.... By the author of
She Caught the Sheriff.

#760 JUST ONE NIGHT • Kathryn Shay
9 Months Later
Annie and Zach Sloan had married for all the right reasons.
They'd fallen in love and neither could imagine life without
the other. But those reasons hadn't been enough to keep
them together. Then—six years after the divorce—a night
that began in fear ended in passion. And now there's a
new reason for Zach and Annie to marry. *They're about to
become parents.*

#761 THIS CHILD IS MINE • Janice Kaiser
Carolina Prescott is pregnant. Webb Harper is the father.
After his wife died, he forgot all about the donation he'd left
at a fertility clinic. Due to a mix-up, Lina is given the wrong
fertilized egg—but that doesn't make her less of a mother!
Both Lina and Webb have strong feelings about the baby
she's carrying and the ensuing lawsuit. Can their growing
feelings for each other overcome the trauma of the battle
for custody?

Take 4 bestselling love stories FREE

Plus get a FREE surprise gift!

Special Limited-time Offer

Mail to Harlequin Reader Service®

3010 Walden Avenue
P.O. Box 1867
Buffalo, N.Y. 14240-1867

YES! Please send me 4 free Harlequin Temptation® novels and my free surprise gift. Then send me 4 brand-new novels every month, which I will receive before they appear in bookstores. Bill me at the low price of $2.90 each plus 25¢ delivery and applicable sales tax, if any.* That's the complete price and a savings of over 10% off the cover prices—quite a bargain! I understand that accepting the books and gift places me under no obligation ever to buy any books. I can always return a shipment and cancel at any time. Even if I never buy another book from Harlequin, the 4 free books and the surprise gift are mine to keep forever.

142 BPA A3UP

Name _____ (PLEASE PRINT)

Address _____ Apt. No. _____

City _____ State _____ Zip _____

This offer is limited to one order per household and not valid to present Harlequin Temptation® subscribers. *Terms and prices are subject to change without notice. Sales tax applicable in N.Y.

UTEMP-696   ©1990 Harlequin Enterprises Limited

HARLEQUIN WOMEN KNOW ROMANCE WHEN THEY SEE IT.

And they'll see it on **ROMANCE CLASSICS**, the new 24-hour TV channel devoted to romantic movies and original programs like the special **Romantically Speaking—Harlequin™ Goes Prime Time.**

Romantically Speaking—Harlequin™ Goes Prime Time introduces you to many of your favorite romance authors in a program developed exclusively for Harlequin® readers.

Watch for **Romantically Speaking—Harlequin™ Goes Prime Time** beginning in the summer of 1997.

If you're not receiving ROMANCE CLASSICS, call your local cable operator or satellite provider and ask for it today!

ROMANCE CLASSICS

Escape to the network of your dreams.

See Ingrid Bergman and Gregory Peck in *Spellbound* on Romance Classics.

NEW ORLEANS KNIGHTS

JOANN ROSS

Three Brothers,
Three Heroes,
Three unforgettable Temptation novels
that will make you stay up past your bedtime...
then dream all through the night....

Don't miss the last book in this amazing series.

MICHAEL: THE DEFENDER #654

Available in October 1997
wherever Harlequin books are sold.

HARLEQUIN®

Temptation.

Look us up on-line at: http://www.romance.net

NOK

Free Gift Offer

With a Free Gift proof-of-purchase
from any Harlequin® book, you can receive
a beautiful cubic zirconia pendant.

This stunning marquise-shaped stone is a genuine cubic
zirconia—accented by an 18" gold tone necklace.
(Approximate retail value $19.95)

Send for yours today...
compliments of ◈HARLEQUIN®

To receive your free gift, a cubic zirconia pendant, send us one original proof-of-purchase, photocopies not accepted, from the back of any Harlequin Romance®, Harlequin Presents®, Harlequin Temptation®, Harlequin Superromance®, Harlequin Intrigue®, Harlequin American Romance®, or Harlequin Historicals® title available at your favorite retail outlet, together with the Free Gift Certificate, plus a check or money order for $1.65 U.S./$2.15 CAN. (do not send cash) to cover postage and handling, payable to Harlequin Free Gift Offer. We will send you the specified gift. Allow 6 to 8 weeks for delivery. Offer good until December 31, 1997, or while quantities last. Offer valid in the U.S. and Canada only.

Free Gift Certificate

Name: _____

Address: _____

City: _____ State/Province: _____ Zip/Postal Code: _____

Mail this certificate, one proof-of-purchase and a check or money order for postage and handling to: HARLEQUIN FREE GIFT OFFER 1997. In the U.S.: 3010 Walden Avenue, P.O. Box 9071, Buffalo NY 14269-9057. In Canada: P.O. Box 604, Fort Erie, Ontario L2Z 5X3.

FREE GIFT OFFER   084-KEZ

ONE PROOF-OF-PURCHASE
To collect your fabulous FREE GIFT, a cubic zirconia pendant, you must include this
original proof-of-purchase for each gift with the properly completed Free Gift Certificate.

084-KEZR